JOE HUSTLE

JOE HUSTLE

A NOVEL

RICHARD LANGE

MULHOLLAND BOOKS

LITTLE, BROWN AND COMPANY

NEW YORK BOSTON LONDON

Hachette Book Group supports the right to free expression and the value of copyright. The purpose of copyright is to encourage writers and artists to produce the creative works that enrich our culture.

The scanning, uploading, and distribution of this book without permission is a theft of the author's intellectual property. If you would like permission to use material from the book (other than for review purposes), please contact permissions@hbgusa.com. Thank you for your support of the author's rights.

Mulholland Books / Little, Brown and Company
Hachette Book Group
1290 Avenue of the Americas, New York, NY 10104
littlebrown.com

First Edition: June 2024

Mulholland Books is an imprint of Little, Brown and Company, a division of Hachette Book Group, Inc. The Mulholland Books name and logo are trademarks of Hachette Book Group, Inc.

The publisher is not responsible for websites (or their content) that are not owned by the publisher.

The Hachette Speakers Bureau provides a wide range of authors for speaking events. To find out more, go to hachettespeakersbureau.com or email hachettespeakers@hbgusa.com.

Little, Brown and Company books may be purchased in bulk for business, educational, or promotional use. For information, please contact your local bookseller or the Hachette Book Group Special Markets Department at special.markets@hbgusa.com.

Excerpt from "Dreaming," written by Eric Bachmann, © 2015 Red Pig Publishing. Used by permission.
Excerpt from "21 Pages" by Robert Lax, from *33 POEMS,* copyright ©1988 by Robert Lax and the Editor. Reprinted by permission of New Directions Publishing Corp.

ISBN 9780316568470
Library of Congress Control Number: 2024935352

Printing 1, 2024

MRQ

Printed in Canada

For Kim Turner

All joy and all desire, for my being,
Are held in you as heat within flame.
— *Tosca,* Act 3

Hey, love, don't turn on me now
I was gonna fight for you.
                    —Eric Bachmann, "Dreaming"

Movement of dark things in darkness,
looking for order.
Looking for some relief from total, all but
total, chaos. Dark
things moving in darkness, trying to find
some kind of
adjustment, some form of order. I look
into the dark and see
darkness, no more light than at the half-
imagined edges of these
dark objects. Darkness made up of objects
slowly turning,
jostling and turning, slowly turning,
trying to discover some
kind of accord.
                    —"21 Pages" by Robert Lax

JOE
HUSTLE

1: GO DODGERS

Junior says he's had enough of Joe's excuses: If he doesn't come up with some cash by Friday, he'll be out on his ass. Joe thinks this is unfair for a number of reasons.

First off, two hundred a week for what's essentially a closet is bullshit.

Second, it's not cool for Junior to be so money-hungry. It was only luck that he inherited his grandmother's house, where he now gets off on playing Filipinotown slumlord, renting out rooms in the dump for way more than they're worth.

Third, even with all the money he's taking in, he still hits Joe up for ten bucks here or twenty bucks there with no intention of paying him back, and after six months of this, Joe feels he's owed at least a bit of grace.

"And now this fucker Paulo, this Brazilian, moved into the room next to mine," Joe tells Mexican Mike, the two of them hunched over the bar at the Lotus Lounge. "He's always

3

watching porn when I'm trying to sleep, and I have to pound on the wall to get him to turn it down. I complained to Junior, but he said he doesn't get involved in tenant disputes."

"Tenant disputes," Mike says.

"In a fucking flophouse," Joe says.

"Flophouse."

Joe realizes that Mike's not listening, just repeating words to make it seem like he is. The dude's been drinking since noon and has more beer than blood in him at this point.

"Anybody want to sing?" the new karaoke guy, Felix, calls out.

The only other people in the joint are Nita the bartender, who's staring at her phone, and Hoon, who's even drunker than Mike, so Felix sings himself, belting out "Footloose" like he's on a TV show.

Tacked to the wall behind the bar are a hundred or so faded and fading photos of customers drinking, singing, and goofing off. Joe spots two dead people without even trying, old Fred and a woman everyone called Mama. He's only been coming here a few months, and already two regulars have kicked the bucket. There's a picture of him, too, posing with a young couple from Norway who wandered in one night from their motel up Vermont. He looks like an old man next to them, older than forty-one, an old drunk slurring nonsense and waving a beer bottle. Maybe he'll be dead soon too.

Mike's asleep now, his forehead propped in his hand. A strand of drool stretches from his lips to the bar. Why wake him? Why bring him back to this? Joe shakes out a Marlboro and lights up instead.

"What you doing?" Nita screeches in her thick Thai accent. "Outside! Outside!"

"Fuck you," Joe says. She doesn't deserve it, but there you go.

He gets up and walks out the door.

Maybe he's hungry. He heads for Jack in the Box. The sun's going down, and the sky is blooming like a rose, turning every shade of pink and orange and purple. People take pictures, and an old woman on a bus bench yells, "*Que maravillosa, que maravillosa!*"

I should be soaking this up too, Joe thinks, and forces himself to stop and watch the show. *Every sunset is the same, but each one is different,* he thinks, and wonders if it's something he heard in a song. Even if it is, at least his brain is still working, which is good to know. He's been feeling stupid lately.

Waiting for his cheeseburger, he texts Matt, who, if he's scheming to rack up enough trips to earn a bonus from Uber, sometimes lets Joe drive his car and use his account.

You been drinking? Matt texts back.

Not yet

K. You can drive till 3. 50%

75

Take it or leave it

I keep my tips

Night spreads over the city as Joe hoofs it to East Hollywood. Matt's block is lined with apartment buildings from the 1930s that look like they belong in New York. A film crew has the street cordoned off. They've set up lights and cameras and piled fake snow on the sidewalk. Joe joins a crowd watching the filming from behind a barricade. A machine spews more snow, someone yells, "Action," and two actors in suits and fedoras leap out of an old-timey car and run into one of the buildings.

"They're paying me five hundred dollars to keep my windows shut," an Armenian guy holding a baby says to Joe.

"You should ask for more in this heat," Joe says.

It's been over a hundred degrees for a week and doesn't cool down at night. The air's a greasy slop of carbon monoxide and festering garbage, and transformers keep blowing and blacking out whole neighborhoods. Everyone's miserable, everyone's pissed off, everyone's desperate for relief.

"Maybe they'll let the kids play in the snow," the Armenian says.

"That's not snow, that's chemicals," Joe tells him.

The production's craft services tent fills the parking lot next to Matt's building. While waiting to be buzzed in, Joe watches a pretty girl eat a bagel. He worked craft services for a while. It was long hours but good pay. He messed up, though, by screwing the boss's wife, losing a sweet gig for a fuck he was too drunk to remember the next day.

Matt's elevator is out of order, and Joe gets a sweat going climbing to his third-floor apartment. A bedroom, wood floors, big windows. He must be paying two grand a month at least.

Framed movie posters cover the walls. *The Dark Knight, Pulp Fiction, John Wick*. Matt's twenty-eight years old. He came from Chicago to write screenplays but spends all his time driving in order to make enough money to survive. Joe met him at the Frolic Room on Hollywood Boulevard. After an hour of listening to him recount the plots of his favorite *Breaking Bad* episodes, Joe said, "You say you're a writer, but all you're telling me are TV shows. Tell me about your *life*."

"My life's boring," Matt said.

"You should write about me then," Joe said. "I was in the Marines, almost got killed in Iraq. I was in prison for a while. My dad shot his brother."

Matt was intrigued. They smoked some crack and worked out a deal where Joe would tell him all the crazy stuff that had happened to him, and Matt would turn it into screenplays. If anything sold, they'd split the money. For a month or so they got together a couple times a week so Matt could record Joe's stories. Nothing came of it, and now, a year later, they only see each other when Joe drives the guy's car.

Matt hands him the fob for his Prius.

"Take it to a car wash first," he says. "A bird shit all over it."

His girlfriend—Mya, Myra—is watching TV on the couch. She hasn't even acknowledged Joe. This pisses Joe off. She thinks shaking her ass in a G-string at Jumbo's for tourists and slumming squares makes her something special.

"How's it going?" Joe says to her.

She rolls her eyes, and Matt laughs.

"She thinks you're creepy," he says. "Old and creepy."

"So you're scared of me," Joe says to the girl.

"You don't even exist," she says.

"Oh, I exist," Joe says. "I exist way more than you exist."

Matt laughs again. He reeks of weed. "She's a fucking diva," he says. "Forget it."

"Divas are supposed to be good at something," Joe says. "What are you good at besides being a bitch?"

"Get this fucking loser out of here," the girl says. "He can't talk to me that way."

Matt steers Joe to the door. "Have the car back by three," he says.

Joe sees himself snatching one of the movie posters off the wall and smashing it over Matt's head, then smashing another over the girl's. If it was ten years ago, there'd be blood and broken glass everywhere.

He drives a chick with green hair to Echo Park, two gay guys downtown, and a rich old hippie couple out to Venice. Two hours in he's made forty bucks.

The dude he picks up next—Asian, thirtyish, drunk—has a cast on his left leg. Joe helps him into the back seat and stows his crutches in the trunk. He's going to Koreatown. After asking Joe to put the Dodger game on the radio, he starts giving directions different from the route Waze plotted. Rule number one is never trust a passenger's directions, especially if the passenger is drunk, but the guy's adamant, so Joe gets off the 10 and takes Olympic.

The guy, Dave, alternates between texting furiously and yelling about the game. It's the bottom of the ninth, and if the Dodgers win, he'll hit a parlay for over a thousand dollars. "Come on, Kenley, strike this motherfucker out!" he screams.

One down, two down, three. Dave explodes, pounding on the back of Joe's seat and yelling, "Go Dodgers!"

"Bro, bro, bro, I'm so happy right now," he says.

"Winning's cool," Joe says.

"I never win."

When they arrive at Dave's destination, a two-story apartment building curled around a small pool, he asks Joe to help him up the stairs to the second floor. Joe is reluctant—the trip has already taken nine minutes longer than it would have if he'd followed Waze—but he doesn't want to risk the dude giving him a low rating.

He retrieves Dave's crutches and walks with him to the entrance of the complex. Dave yells through the gate to a guy sitting by the pool, "I'm Chloe in 208's boyfriend. Can you let me in?"

The guy opens the gate. When they get to the stairs, Dave hands Joe the crutches and uses the banister to pull himself up, one awkward step at a time. Joe stays close, ready to catch him, but he makes it to the top without falling.

"I'm only gonna be here five minutes," he says. "I'll give

you fifty dollars if you wait and drive me to the bar I'm going to next."

Fifty bucks free and clear sounds good, so Joe follows him down the walkway to an apartment overlooking the pool. Dave feels along the top of the doorframe and checks under the mat. He finally finds a key buried in the soil of a potted palm.

"Come in and have a drink," he says. "She's a bartender, so everything's top shelf."

The apartment is spotless. It even smells clean. Nice furniture, nice lamps, nice magazines. The booze is on the kitchen counter. Jack Daniel's, Patron, Grey Goose. Dave takes two glasses from a rack next to the sink. He pours a slug of Jack into one, downs it, and pours another.

"What your pleasure?" he asks Joe.

"Jack's good," Joe says. He tries to stop Dave when the glass is a quarter full, but the guy keeps pouring.

"I'll finish what you don't," he says.

Dave looks through the cupboards and pulls out a box of Ritz crackers. He takes a bottle of ketchup from the refrigerator.

"Hang here," he says, and leaves the kitchen.

Joe sips his whiskey. How many more trips can he clock before three? A giggle prompts him to step into the living room and peek down the hall. Dave's in the bedroom. He's pulled back the bed's duvet and is crumbling crackers onto the sheets. He squirts ketchup over the crackers.

"What the fuck are you up to?" Joe says.

"It's a joke on my girlfriend," Dave replies.

He takes a picture of the mess and sends it to someone.

"I gotta go," Joe says.

"Drink your drink."

Dave's phone rings. He puts the call on speaker.

"That's right, bitch," he says.

"I called the police," a girl says. "They're on their way."

"I don't give a fuck," Dave says. He unzips his jeans and pisses on the bed.

Joe hurries out the door and sprints down the stairs. He's pretty sure he could talk himself out of trouble with the cops, but he doesn't need them running his license and finding something he's forgotten about. He hops into the Prius and speeds away to the warble of approaching sirens. That's what you get for helping people. All of a sudden you're an accomplice.

July 12, 11:45 p.m.

Okay, I'm recording.

Ask me something.

Where were you born?

[Laughter] Seriously?

Just tell me a story.

I was born in Burbank. Hand me another beer. In Burbank. We lived in an apartment on Verdugo, then
moved to a house on Parish. By Burroughs High.

That's not a story. What kind of shenanigans did you get
up to when you were a kid?

Shenanigans? [Laughter] You kids and your shenanigans.

What kind of shit? What kind of trouble?

I started drinking when I was twelve, started smoking
weed, dropped a ton of acid. Me and my friends basi-
cally lived at this park on Olive. None of our parents
gave a shit. This one time I was tripping my brains out
there. It was midnight, and I was laying on a picnic
table, looking for UFOs. I used to do that all the time,
be like, "Come and get me. Take me with you." Sending an SOS into space.

Did you ever see any?

What?

UFOs.

Fuck yeah. Tons.

Aliens?

You want to hear this or not? I was laying on the table,
and I heard heavy breathing, like something big, some

11

big animal, was right there. Did you ever stand next to a horse, or, like, an elephant?

I grew up in Chicago, man. Where do they have elephants in Chicago?

At the zoo. They let you pet them on field trips and shit. That's what it sounded like, like an elephant breathing. Tons of air going in and tons of air whooshing out. I turned my head to look, and what I saw…Check out my arm—goose bumps, twenty-five years later. What I saw was— BOO! Ha! Got you! You fucking jumped.

Is this a stupid campfire story?

Nah, nah, I'm being serious. I turned my head and saw this thing. A black shadow, ten feet tall. It didn't have eyes, but I could tell it was staring at me. I wanted to yell, but I couldn't. I wanted to run, but my legs wouldn't work.

Maybe you were dreaming. Maybe you fell asleep.

I wasn't asleep.

But you *were* tripping.

I know what tripping is. This had nothing to do with tripping. This was something super freaky. This thing walked over and put its hand on my chest, and it was so cold, it burned. I passed out, and when I came to, whatever it was was gone.

How long were you out?

Not long. A few minutes. I got up and rode my bike home as fast as I could.

Maybe it was an alien. Maybe your message got through.

It wasn't an alien.

A ghost then.

I told this goth chick about it, and she said it sounded like
   a demon, but I think it was Death himself. Death was
   coming for me, but something stopped him.
What? What stopped him?
I think I've got a light in me. I've come so close to getting killed so many times, done so much stupid shit
   and survived, I think I've got a light in me that's stronger than death.

2: RIDE THE LIGHTNING

Joe's been up and down so many times, it makes him seasick to think about it. Whenever he manages to save a few bucks and get a decent place to live or a reliable vehicle, something happens to send him to the bottom of the hill again. He crawled his way out of the gutter after being released from Chino, was working for a painting contractor, had an apartment in North Hollywood, a truck, some furniture. But then his boss got caught selling stolen goods, and there went that. Joe couldn't find work anywhere else, lost the apartment and the furniture, and ended up sleeping in the truck until he lost that too.

A few years later he was back on track again, thanks to a steady bartending gig at McRed's, a dive in Van Nuys. Same deal: apartment, truck, TV. Two years passed, and he was starting to save for a down payment on a condo. The owner of the bar made some bad investments, though—at the blackjack table, on the high-limit slots—and had to lay off most of the staff, Joe included. Joe blew through his unemployment, couldn't get work that paid enough, and ended that slide bunking in a friend's garage.

His most recent roller-coaster ride started when he scored a job tending bar at a place in Echo Park, the Short Stop. After working there a while he had his ducks in a row again but got into it with the manager over a car she sold him, a Volkswagen Bug that blew up the second time he drove it. The dispute turned ugly, and the bar's owner took the manager's side and fired Joe.

That was a year ago, and he's been on the hustle ever since, taking whatever work he can get, moving from couch to couch, from shitty furnished room to shitty furnished room, no car, no stuff, no safety net. He usually manages to string together enough gigs to make his nut, but this month he got lazy. He just couldn't deal with all the texting, all the phone calls, all the *begging* it takes to keep his head above water. All he wanted to do was drink, smoke weed, and sleep. And now here he is, close to flat broke and about to be evicted.

He goes into panic mode, hitting up everyone he knows for jobs. Keith gets right back to him, saying he'll give him a hundred bucks to help him paint a house if he can be in Los Feliz in an hour. Keith has a good thing going: Rich people who don't like dealing with Mexicans will pay a premium for a white painter, and he's their man. He smiles down from his ladder when Joe arrives at the house almost two hours later.

"I know I'm late, but the bus broke down," Joe says. "Check it out though: I'm gonna give you my phone to hold. That way I won't be tempted to look at it, and I'll be able to give you a thousand percent."

"You don't have to do that," Keith says.

"No, man, I do. I want to."

Keith locks the phone in his black F-150 and sets Joe up with a cordless sander, a mask, and a ladder. His job is to prep some siding on the back of the house, removing as much of the old paint as possible. It's grunt work, hot, dirty, and boring. Sweat mixes with dust to muddy Joe's sunglasses, and he tosses the mask because it makes him feel like he's suffocating. If all the poison he's run through his lungs thus far hasn't killed him, a little lead paint surely won't.

The house is a Tudor fantasia from the thirties with a pool and small guesthouse. Joe can see the Hollywood sign from atop his ladder. After a couple hours he begins to regret surrendering his phone. What if he misses a call about a real job?

Keith appears and asks if he brought water.

"I didn't have time to stop," Joe says.

"There's a cooler in my truck," Keith says. "Make sure you stay hydrated."

As soon as he says this, Joe realizes he's parched. He descends the ladder, cleans his sunglasses as best he can with his sweaty T-shirt, and walks out front to the F-150. The cooler's in the bed. Joe guzzles one bottle of water and rolls another across his forehead. He can see his phone on the passenger seat. He tries the door, but it's locked. The driver's side too.

He returns to the backyard and sits on a chaise to drink the second bottle of water. He's listening to bees buzz and watching the pool skimmer make its rounds when he feels eyes on him. A coyote is staring from an overgrown corner of the yard. Joe yells and waves his arms, but instead of fleeing the animal walks to the pool and laps at the water. You don't usually see them in the middle of the day, which makes Joe worry this one might have rabies or something. He yells again.

The door to the guesthouse opens, and a woman steps out, curious about the hubbub.

"Careful," Joe calls to her. "Coyote."

"Holy shit," the woman says, backing up.

Joe grabs a broom leaning against the wall of the house and cautiously makes his way around the pool. "Git!" he yells. The coyote stops drinking and stares at him again. Joe slaps the broom on the surface of the water. "Git!" The animal bolts for the rear of the property, and Joe follows.

"Don't hurt him," the woman says.

The coyote scrambles onto the brick ruins of an old fireplace, glances once more at Joe, then hops over the fence and disappears into a stand of bamboo in the neighbor's yard.

"He comes around all the time," the woman says.

"Better keep your cats inside," Joe says.

"Too late."

Joe gives the woman a look.

"Joking," she says. "Sorry."

She could be anywhere from thirty to forty. Not thin, not heavy, five-six, five-seven, curvaceous. Her dark, curly hair is cut short, which makes her big brown eyes look even bigger, and she's got a bright smile and expressive lips. Her whole face is expressive. Joe feels like he could read her every thought there if she wasn't careful. She's barefoot and wearing cutoff jean shorts and a Metallica T-shirt that Joe's sure is another joke.

"You could make the fence higher," he says. "An extra foot would keep him out."

"I'll tell my sister," the woman says. "It's her house."

"Lucky her."

"She's an attorney. She's got all the money in the whole wide world."

Joe gestures at the woman's shirt. "Name one Metallica song."

The woman pulls the shirt away from her body and looks at it like she's never seen it before. "I didn't bring enough clothes, so I pulled this out of a drawer," she says. "Are they your favorite or something?"

"I liked them when I was a kid," Joe says.

"But now you're into classical, right? That's why you've got all the tattoos?"

Feeling self-conscious, Joe glances at the junk ink that's accumulated on his hands and arms over the years. "Beethoven might be in there somewhere," he says. "You don't have any?"

"Not yet," the woman says.

Keith calls to him from the pool deck. "I need your help with something out front."

"You're gonna get me in trouble," Joe whispers to the woman.

"Don't blame me," she says.

Joe joins Keith, spieling about the coyote as he goes. "It was fricking huge." He's sly about watching the woman go back inside the guesthouse. She'll be the highlight of his day for sure. Everything's been so goddamn ugly lately, he'd forgotten there were pretty things like her in the world.

When he and Keith finish unloading a bunch of five-gallon buckets of paint from the truck, Joe finally cracks and asks for his phone. There's a text from Wahid wondering if he's free to work at his family's liquor store tonight. *Absolutely,* Joe replies.

He and Keith knock off at four. Keith asks if he's free tomorrow, says he can use him the whole day.

"I appreciate it," Joe says. "My landlord's breathing down my neck."

A silver Discovery pulls into the driveway and parks next to

Keith's truck. The woman who gets out resembles the woman from the guesthouse but older and grouchy. She nods at Joe and Keith. The teenagers with her, a boy and a girl, don't look up from their phones.

"How's it going?" the woman asks.

"We're right on schedule," Keith says.

"Awesome," the woman says, already thinking about something else. She follows the kids up the steps to the front door of the house.

"Just so you know, there was a coyote in the backyard earlier," Joe says.

"Yeah, they're a problem around here," the woman says.

"I showed your sister where it came over the fence. If you want, I can build it up there so it'll be too high for them to jump."

"How much would that cost?"

"I'll do it for a hundred bucks plus the lumber."

"Sure, go for it," the woman says, and walks into the house.

Keith shakes his head. "Fucking Joe Hustle," he says.

"Got my mind on my money and my money on my mind," Joe replies.

July 22, 10:05 p.m.

I was chasing a pint a day with a twelve-pack and snorting all the coke I could afford. I wanted to clean up and figured the Corps would be a good place to do it, so I enlisted.

And they took you?

This was in 2001. They were taking anybody, getting ready for the shit that was about to go down. I sobered up enough to pass the piss test and was in.

Did it work?

What?

Did you clean up?

I did pretty good my first year, until we went over to Iraq. My regiment was one of the first across the border.

Awesome. Tell me a war story. A good one.

There's no good war stories, bro.

3: HOW TO GET
TO HEAVEN

Keith gives Joe a ride to Junior's and says he'll be back to pick him up in the morning. When it was built in 1910, the big two-story Craftsman was one of the nicest houses on the block. Now it's a wreck, the foundation cracked, the frame made flimsy by termites and dry rot. The cheap apartment buildings that surround it went up in the sixties and seventies. They used to be full of Filipinos, but these days it's Guatemalans, Salvadorians, and Hondurans. Late at night Joe hears the old house groan, ready to lay down its burden, ready to fall in on itself and get some rest.

Robert and Candy are smoking weed on the porch, lazing on a cracked vinyl couch. They rent a room on the first floor. One or the other might be on the run.

"You look like a working man," Robert says. "God bless working men." He offers Joe the joint.

"Nah, I'm gonna be in and out," Joe says.

Candy strums a ukulele. "Working man," she sings. "Working man. Kissing the ass of the ruling class."

Stepping into the house is like stepping into an oven. Joe feels like he's struggling to breathe through a rag tied over his nose and mouth. Junior is lying shirtless on the living room floor in front of a big industrial fan. He weighs three hundred pounds, and his tits sag like an old woman's.

"Got my money?" he says.

Joe hands him sixty dollars and promises more tomorrow.

Junior sits up and holds out a machete. "Look at this."

"I've got to grab a shower and get going," Joe says.

"Come on, check it out."

Joe takes the machete and swings it back and forth.

"That's a *barong*," Junior says. "Weapon of choice for Moro suicide fighters in the Philippines during the rebellion against the Americans."

Junior's family has been in the U.S. for a hundred years, but lately he's been getting in touch with his heritage. A few months ago he took to wearing a pointy straw hat he bought at a Philippine cultural festival, said it was the traditional hat of his people, and now it's this machete.

"Suicide fighters?" Joe says.

"Crazy fucking Muslims," Junior says. "They charged the American riflemen carrying just these blades after wrapping rope around their arms and legs to slow the bleeding in case they got shot. Fucking badasses, bro. Fucking jihad."

You don't know shit about jihad, Joe thinks. He hands back the machete and asks Junior what he's going to do with it.

"You can do a million things with a machete," Junior says.

Joe's room is on the second floor of the house, up a creaking staircase. He unlocks the padlock that secures the door. The room is eight feet by twelve. Big enough some days, nowhere near big enough others. The single tiny window looks out on the pink stucco of the apartment building next door. The bed, dresser, card table, and folding chair were here when he moved in. He's proud of not needing anything more, proud that everything he owns fits into a backpack.

He turns on a fan to stir the hot air and gathers up his kit bag, towel, and a clean shirt and jeans. The door to the bathroom down the hall is locked, somebody in there, so he has to shower in the one downstairs. The tub, toilet, and floor are disgusting. Junior has a maid in once a month, but that's not often enough with eight people living, cooking, and shitting in one place. The secret is not to focus on anything. You have to get in and get out without looking too closely at whatever the hell that is on the tile next to the toilet. The hot water runs out while he's washing his hair.

Returning to the second floor, he hears a door open as he reaches the top step. He peeks around the corner to see Janey the Jesus Freak, who lives in the room at the end of the hall, come out of the bathroom. Janey watches fire-and-brimstone preachers on TV and slides tracts with titles like "How to Get to Heaven" and "Now the End Begins" under everyone's doors. Any conversation with her turns into a sermon, so Joe waits until she's in her room before going to his.

He opens a can of tuna. He keeps his food in his room, cold stuff in a foam cooler, because the house is full of thieves. The ice in the cooler has melted, but his Diet Cokes haven't gotten too warm yet. He drinks one with his sandwich, Fritos, and banana.

After he finishes eating, he carries the cooler down to the kitchen, fills it with ice from the filthy refrigerator, and takes it back up to his room. Robert and Candy are with Junior in the living room when he heads out. They're watching a show about people who live in the Alaskan wilderness, Robert idly waving the machete over his head.

"Later, Joe," they all say like it's some kind of shared joke.

Joe splurges on an Uber to Wahid's liquor store. It's on Sixth east of MacArthur Park, next to a steam-table Chinese restaurant with a health department rating of C. A steel grate plastered with ads for Tecate and Marlboro protects the front window.

Wahid's behind the counter. His family came from Pakistan twenty years ago, when he was twelve. Joe met him when they were both doing phone sales, pushing solar setups out of a boiler room in Glendale. Wahid was also clerking at the family store and driving a taxi, and Joe was bartending at night. They bonded over the fact that they were both hustlers, and kept in touch after the boiler room shut down. Wahid eventually began giving Joe occasional shifts at the store.

Wahid is wearing a dress shirt and tie this evening and has his Pakistani music turned up loud. "My friend, good to see you," he says to Joe.

"What's happening?" Joe says. "You getting married?"

Four more Pakistanis, dressed up like Wahid, spill out of the stockroom, laughing and singing along to the song that's playing.

"It's my mother's birthday," Wahid says. "My nephew was supposed to work, but he's sick. Thank you for coming in."

"Anytime," Joe says.

"Here are my cousins from San Diego. Guys, this is my buddy Joe."

"Hey, Joe, where you going with that gun in your hand?" one of the cousins sings.

Wahid says he'll be back around midnight. He follows his cousins out to a minivan parked in front of the store. They're all still singing as the van drives away.

Joe turns off the music and settles in behind the register. A TV mounted on the wall above the beer cooler shows the views from four security cameras, three inside the store, one outside. A sign above it says *SMILE*.

A man comes in and buys a quart of Olde English. A girl pushing a stroller uses an EBT card to pay for half a gallon of milk and some Flaming Hot Cheetos and counts out nickels and dimes from a Ziploc bag for diapers.

Between customers Joe plays poker on his phone. He used to watch tournaments on TV and got to thinking it might be an easy way to make some money. He started going to Commerce and playing low-stakes hold 'em, but every time he sat down at a table, he got his ass handed to him. Playing there wasn't like playing with friends. Everyone was so goddamn serious, telling him to shut up whenever he made a joke. And he discovered winning had little to do with luck. It was all about numbers, and he has no head for numbers. He also might have done better if he hadn't drunk so much while playing.

He sells a pint of whiskey, a pint of tequila, two cans of beans, a dozen tortillas, and a jar of instant coffee. And lottery tickets. Lots of lottery tickets. Scratchers, Powerball, Super-Lotto, Fantasy Five.

An old man in a Dodgers cap steps up to the counter and says, "Cuatro."

"Cuatro what?" Joe says.

"Where's Wahid?"

"It's his mom's birthday."

"He knows what I want."

"Well, he's not here."

The old man blinks his watery red eyes. The wrinkles on his face look like furrows left by a rake drawn through dust. "Four of them little vodkas," he finally says. Joe grabs four Smirnoffs from a display of airplane bottles. "And one of the dollar scratchers."

The old man methodically scrapes the ticket with the edge of a quarter. As each number is revealed, he brings the ticket close to his eyes and squints to see if it's a match. Not tonight.

At ten Joe steps outside for a cigarette, smokes it standing in the doorway. Another hot summer night like this one comes back to him so clearly he flinches, another night when he stood smoking in a doorway, fluorescent light behind him, watching traffic roll past. He was young then, and happy about something, but that's all he remembers. Couldn't tell you what street, what year. These moments when the time line of his life doubles back and crosses itself always come out of nowhere, sucker punches.

A speed freak scuttles toward him, a little zombie girl looking over her shoulder and mumbling to herself, tugging at her oversize Minnie Mouse T-shirt and swiping at the black tears crawling down her cheeks.

"Can I use your bathroom?" she asks. She walks in a circle, stuck in fifth gear.

"It's out of order," Joe lies.

"Let me have a cigarette."

"This is my last one."

The girl scoffs at this and zooms off down the sidewalk, collides with a woman carrying a basket of laundry, screeches, whirls, and disappears around the corner.

Joe sells beer and a bag of chips; beer and Gatorade; beer, a bar of soap, and a pack of tube socks. A woman asks if he'll

break a hundred. No bills over twenty. He IDs a kid for cigarettes and gets told to fuck off. Around eleven he's staring at
the TV above the cooler and sees someone tagging the Tecate
banner outside. He runs out and chases the asshole off.

Things slow down after that. He plays more poker. He spins
a quarter on the counter, clocking how long he can get it to
go before it falls. Wahid returns at twelve-fifteen with one of
his cousins. They're both drunk.

"Everything cool?" Wahid asks.

"Nothing too crazy," Joe replies.

Wahid gives him a hundred in twenties and says to take a
pint of whatever he wants. He walks back to Junior's, cracks
the Wild Turkey on the way. Everyone's still out on the street,
trying to cool down. Old folks gossiping, kids riding scooters,
teenagers groping against cars. Tonight, Joe loves them all.
Whiskey's good that way sometimes.

July 19, 12:45 a.m.

I'm the son of a violent man.
So you're saying you were fucked from the jump.
I'm saying nothing but crows come out of a crow's nest.
That's awesome. I'm stealing that.
Here's another one: If one dog howls a lie, ten thousand
    dogs will pass it on as the truth.
All right! Fucking Confucius. Fucking Socrates.

4: DON'T DIE!

Joe rolls a coat of paint onto the back wall of the house, then switches to a brush for the detail work. The daughter of the home's owner is sprawled in an orange bikini on a chaise by the pool. She's older than Joe thought she was yesterday but still young enough that he feels pervy sneaking peeks. She answers a phone call with "What up, ho?" and the conversation that follows mystifies Joe. The girl and whoever she's talking to seem to be speaking in code, like he and his friends did in high school, referring to dope as CDs in order to fool the narcs they fantasized were listening in on their calls. "Got any CDs, dude?"

He wonders if the owner's sister is inside the guesthouse. He's been reluctant to look over that way in case she's watching from behind the curtains. She could be. She was flirting some yesterday, and he might be popping into her head like she's been popping into his.

"Toodles," the daughter says to end her call. "Buy those shoes."

A pair of finches tussle in a magenta-flowered bougainvillea. Joe spots a nest on the ground next to the bush, a tiny basket woven of dry grass, twigs, and a length of red string that courses through it like a vein. There are no eggs in it, so he decides to keep it rather than reseat it among the thorny branches. He stows it next to his bottle of water.

The girl goes inside the house, and Joe moves to a new section of wall and lays down a first coat. The money he made at the liquor store last night and what he'll earn today will square him with Junior, and Keith said he can use him for another couple days, which should carry him to the end of the month. He's so intent on his calculations he doesn't notice that the owner's sister has come out of the guesthouse and is sitting at the little table in front of its French doors until she says, "Is that No Doubt you're whistling?"

"I was whistling?" he says. "Sorry."

"I didn't take you for a No Doubt kind of dude."

"Make a request."

"How about some Bowie?"

He trills a bit of "Rebel Rebel," which makes the woman smile. He likes her smile. Pointing at the book in her hand, he says, "What are you reading?"

She shows him the cover.

"I can't even pronounce that," he jokes.

"An-na Ka-ren-ih-na," she says, joking too.

"How long does it take to read a book that thick?" he asks her.

"It's a project," she says. "I always have to have a project."

"Want to see something cool?" he says. He takes the nest over and places it on the table. The woman picks it up and turns it in her hands.

"Wow," she says. "Look how intricate."

"I found a raven's nest once," Joe says. "It was made out of all kinds of random stuff. Wire, bones, fur, a potato chip bag, an old sock. Kinda spooky but kinda neat."

"This one's gorgeous."

"Keep it."

"Come on."

"I found it on your property."

"I love it," she says, rubbing the nest against her cheek like it's a kitten. "What's your name?"

"Joe," Joe says.

"Thanks, Joe. I'm Emily."

They shake hands. Emily flips Joe's to look at the tattoos on his fingers. "What's that say?" she asks.

He puts his fists together to show her. DON'T on the fingers of the right hand, DIE! on the fingers of the left. "It's my motto," he says.

"Snappy," she says. "I like it."

Joe goes back to work but has trouble keeping his mind on the job with Emily sitting there reading. He imagines she's watching him, and finds himself striking poses, trying to look like a real craftsman. *You fucking fool,* he thinks.

He and Keith make a Home Depot run at lunchtime. Some of the house's fascia boards are so termite-damaged, they'll have to be replaced. Keith buys the lumber for that and fronts Joe the money to get the planks he'll need to keep the coyote from coming over the fence.

Joe steps outside for a cigarette while Keith is paying. He likes watching the carts go in empty and come out full and thinking about all the jobs that are going to get done and all the things that are going to be built. A text comes from

Carlos, the owner of the Short Stop, the joint he used to work at in Echo Park. There's a Dodger home game tonight, and someone called in sick. Can he come in? After a year of ass-kissing, he's managed to get back into the good graces of both Carlos and Shannon, the manager he beefed with about the Volkswagen, and they've been giving him a few fill-in shifts a month. *FUCK YEAH!!!* he texts back.

When Keith comes out they drive through McDonald's and park in the lot of the supermarket next door to eat. Keith's son is playing Little League, and Keith's not happy with his coach. He thinks he's too easygoing. He also doesn't like the league's "everybody plays" rule.

"Every player has to bat at least once a game and play somewhere on defense for six outs," he says. "What's that teach them? Even if you suck at something, you still get to play?"

"It's Little League," Joe says. "Shit'll get serious when they get to high school."

"High school's too late if you want to play for a good college or go pro," Keith says. "Cody's super advanced for his age. He's nine but throws like a fourteen-year-old. I'm getting him a private coach and putting him in a real league next year, one that's actually competitive."

Joe never got into sports. He was decent at basketball as a kid but hated being coached, hated following rules, and hated playing on a team. He just wanted to shoot baskets. He spent hours by himself practicing layups, practicing jump shots, but only played in three real games.

"My wife says I'm pushing him," Keith continues. "We got in a big fight about it. If it was up to her, she'd let him sit in front of the computer all day. That's what him and all his friends are into, watching dudes play video games on Twitch.

There's guys making millions doing it. The kids know their names like we used to know ballplayers' names."

"Maybe your wife's onto something," Joe says. "If Cody gets into that, he'll make tons of dough without fucking up his shoulder."

"Over my dead body," Keith says.

They watch a meth fiend dance with a shopping cart, spinning it, bowing to it, spinning it again.

"Do-si-do your corner girl," Joe says.

Keith doesn't crack a smile. He must still be bickering with his wife in his head.

They pull down the old fascia and put up the new. Joe holds the boards in place while Keith nails, then gets back to painting. Emily goes twice from the guesthouse to the main house while he's working. On the first trip, she makes and eats a grilled cheese sandwich, waving to Joe through the slider. The second time she's wearing workout clothes, and Joe hears a yoga class coming from a TV somewhere in the house.

Before he and Keith knock off, he carries the lumber for the fence into the backyard. Emily emerges from the guesthouse again, hair wet from a shower, while he's stacking the wood.

"Finished for the day?" she says.

"Finished here," he says. "I'm bartending tonight."

"Been there, done that," she says.

"You tended bar? Where?"

"Seattle, New Orleans, Miami. That's my go-to survival gig."

"So you don't mind drunks."

"Not if they're tipping."

"You should come down," Joe says. "It's the Short Stop. On Sunset by Dodger Stadium."

"I've been there," Emily says.

"It's fun, right? There's a game tonight, so it'll be pumping. And I make a killer margarita."

"Mine's better."

"Come down and we'll see."

Joe wonders if he's reading her correctly. Some women's codes are hard to crack, especially those of sassy chicks like her.

"Maybe I'll stop by," she says.

"If there's a line, tell the door guy you're there to see Joe Hustle," he says.

"Your last name's Hustle?"

"It's actually McDonald, but everybody calls me Joe Hustle."

"How come?"

"Because I'm always hustling."

Emily makes a face. "That could be a warning," she says.

"Nah, it's a good thing," Joe says.

He looks down at his T-shirt. It's filthy. He hopes Emily doesn't notice.

Keith doesn't have much to say during the ride back to Junior's house, and Joe doesn't try to fill the silence. A Classic Rock Countdown is on the radio, Guns N' Roses's "Welcome to the Jungle" slipping in at number ten.

They get stuck in a traffic jam and inch along until they come to a pickup on fire in the right lane. Black smoke boils out from under the hood and flames sneak into the cab through the dash vents. A guy in a Lakers jersey, maybe the truck's owner, is yelling into a phone and stamping his feet like an angry child.

Keith out of nowhere asks Joe if he can get him some heroin. Joe's thrown for a loop. He had no idea Keith fucked with junk, and he's both angry and ashamed that the guy would think he knows where to score it.

"For you?" he says.

Keith shrugs, embarrassed now himself. "It's the only thing that helps my back when it gets real bad."

Typical junkie bullshit. Joe thinks of the guy's kids and feels sick to his stomach. He's not so much of a hypocrite, though, that he calls him out and tries to split hairs about which drugs are good and which are bad. All he says is "Sorry, bro, can't help you."

Keith comes back with "Cool, cool," but Joe can tell he regrets asking. The silence that fills the truck during the rest of the ride is different from the one before.

When they pull up in front of Junior's, Keith says, "I know I promised you a few more days, but I'm not gonna need you. I can handle the rest myself."

That's fine with Joe. He just wants to get out of the truck as fast as he can.

Keith hands him three hundreds and says, "I appreciate the help."

"Keep me in mind for anything else," Joe says, and bolts for the house.

He gets up to his room and is all of a sudden exhausted, like someone pulled his plug. Too much drama for one day. He strips to his underwear, aims the fan at the bed, and passes out until it's time to get ready for his shift at the bar.

July 22, 10:08 p.m.

We got orders to take a bridge in a city called Nasiriyah, so we loaded up in a bunch of AAVs, what they call tracks, and headed out. Another company and some tanks were supposed to come with us, but things got screwed up, and we ended up going alone, driving right through the middle of town down this street we called Ambush Alley.

That's the title of the movie, for sure.

Sitting in a track is like sitting in a sardine can. You're all crammed together, and there's no windows, so you don't know what the fuck's going on outside. I started hearing *plink plink plink,* like raindrops, rounds hitting our vehicle. *Plink plink plink.* Then all hell broke loose, and we were getting hammered from all sides. Our gunner got hit, so another guy climbed up and took over for him. Our driver was steering with one hand and firing his M-16 with the other. It was so fucking loud, my teeth hurt. I was scared shitless, but I wasn't gonna sit there and wait to get my dick blown off. I opened a hatch and stood on two dudes' shoulders with my SAW. They were shooting at us from every rooftop, every window, every alley, so I let her rip, threw a thousand rounds a minute at anything that moved. Old men, women, kids. This dude stepped out into the street with an RPG, and I cut him in half, literally in two pieces. Rounds were zipping past my head, and I probably would've been killed if something hadn't blown a hole in the side of the track. I fell back down inside, and there was fire everywhere, smoke, screaming. Everyone was slipping and sliding in all the blood on the floor. We kept moving, though, and I don't know how, but the whole convoy made it through the Alley and across the bridge.

Fuck, bro. That was intense. I need another beer.

Get me one too.

[Pause]

So mission accomplished, right? You took the bridge.

Yeah, but you don't get to leave. Take and hold was the order. Take and hold, Marine! We were parked on the bank of the canal the bridge crossed, which made us sitting ducks when the hajis started pounding us with mortars and artillery. We piled out of the tracks and took cover, got our own mortars set up, our machine guns, and radioed for help. The hajis were taking out the tracks one by one and picking us off the same way. After an hour the CO decided to load the wounded into the vehicles that weren't blown to shit and take them back over the bridge and up the Alley to safety.

Seriously?

It was either that or they were all gonna die. We heard a plane coming while we were loading them in, one of ours, a Warthog, and we were like, "Fucking excellent!" but then it opened up on us. Guys were getting hit left and right. The dude next to me's head exploded, and I was picking chunks of him off my vest a week later. We sent flares up to let the Hog know we were Marines, but it made two more passes before it broke off. And then, as the tracks with the wounded were crossing the bridge, another Hog lit *them* up, killing more of our guys.

Friendly fire.

Fuck that. Eighteen guys got killed. They did an investigation afterward and determined the Iraqis got eight of them, but they couldn't tell who killed the others because they had wounds from both haji weapons and the Hogs. They blamed the whole thing on what they called the fog of war, which meant nobody got punished. Nobody except us. We were pinned down by that bridge for three hours before they got us out. For three hours I lay there knowing, just knowing, I was done for.

5: THE MEN THAT DON'T FIT IN

THE SHORT STOP IS ONLY HALF A MILE FROM DODGER STA-dium. Before and after home games, it's packed with fans decked out in blue-and-white jerseys and other team swag. Joe comes on at six. It's him and Bob O'Reilly—Joe calls him Baba—slinging drinks. Shannon, the manager, is also lurk-ing. First pitch is at seven fifteen, so pre-gamers are stacked three deep at the bar when Joe slips behind it. He doesn't even have time to get his bearings before fools are calling out orders. He quickly finds his groove, boogeying up and down his half of the stick, pulling draft PBRs and pouring shots of rotgut tequila. It's work he can lose himself in. He's always appreci-ated that.

The rush dies at seven when everybody staggers up the hill to the stadium. Joe draws himself a beer and gulps it. Baba's got a new haircut. It looks like someone put a bowl on his head and snipped around it. The kid's twenty-three and in a band, so he must know what's cool, but Joe gives him shit anyway.

"What do they call that 'do?" he asks him. "The *Dumb and Dumber?*"

"Take it easy, Gramps," Baba replies.

Shannon's on the smoking patio when Joe steps out for a cigarette. She's a skinny, hatchet-faced blonde who's always looking for a reason to go off.

"What's shaking?" she says.

"Go Dodgers," Joe says. He's convinced she knew the Volkswagen was a lemon and is still pissed about the two grand he threw away on it, but his shifts here are lifesavers, and he learned a long time ago how to fake the friendly in order to keep a good thing going.

"Did you hear both Jules and Raven are quitting?" Shannon asks him.

He heard but pretends he didn't. "I know Jules was thinking about moving to Portland," he says.

"Me and Carlos have been talking about bringing you back full-time, if you're interested," Shannon says.

Joe takes home two hundred bucks on a good night here. Even if they only give him four shifts a week, he'll make enough to move out of Junior's and buy a car, or at least a motorcycle. He doesn't let on to Shannon how eager he is to return, though. She's not someone you want knowing you're desperate. "I've been clerking at a friend's liquor store off and on, but I could work around that," he says.

"We'll figure something out," Shannon says.

Joe's feeling good when he steps back behind the bar. It's about time luck swung his way. "Midnight Rambler" is on the jukebox. He sings to Baba, wiggling like Jagger. X's "Los

Angeles" comes on next, another favorite. A USC sorority girl complains that her greyhound isn't strong enough. Instead of blowing her off, Joe pours her an extra shot.

The place used to be a cop bar. When Carlos remodeled it, he left the wooden lockers where the officers stowed their guns. Some goofballs are taking selfies in front of them. One of them drops a glass that shatters on the floor. Joe alerts Manuel, the barback, who hurries over to clean it up.

Carlos comes in with a crew of flamboyantly dressed hipsters who turn everyone's heads.

"Oh, shit," Baba says. "That's—"

Joe doesn't hear the name over the music. "Who?" he says.

"A super-famous DJ," Baba says. "And that's his girlfriend, that chick from that Netflix show."

Shannon greets the group and follows them to the VIP room. Five minutes later she comes to the bar and orders a bunch of drinks and tells Joe to deliver them to Carlos and his guests.

Joe sets the order up on a tray and walks it back. He punches the code into the lock on the VIP room door and pushes the door open with his shoulder. Everyone except the DJ is sitting on the couches arrayed around a big glass coffee table. The DJ is dancing to the music blasting over the room's speakers, something loud and bassy.

"This here's Joe Hustle," Carlos announces.

"Howdy," Joe says.

"Thank you, sir," the DJ says when Joe hands him his Jack and Coke. He has a German accent and is wearing too much cologne. "I like your tattoo," he says, pointing at the T. rex in a top hat on Joe's forearm. "I want to get one so bad, but I can't handle pain."

"It doesn't hurt that much," Joe says. "Just don't get it in your armpit."

"Armpit?"

Thinking the guy might not know the word in English, Joe points and says, "It's the most painful spot."

"You have a tattoo in your armpit?" the DJ says.

"Not me, but that's what I've heard from people that do," Joe says.

When he gets back to the bar, he tells Baba that DJ Hansel-and-Gretel is a big pussy.

"His name is Lush Life," Baba says.

Joe notices Emily standing at the stick.

"You made it," he says.

"This is the first time I've been out since I got into town," she says.

"Have you ever heard of Lush Life?"

"No."

"Good," Joe says. "I'm not the only one."

She looks fine in her jeans and tank top, a little bit of makeup. Not trying too hard but prettier than ever. Joe directs her to an empty stool and tosses a napkin so that it spins to a stop in front of her.

"Check you out," she says. "I'll have one of your famous margaritas."

Joe shakes up tequila, Cointreau, lime juice, and simple syrup, pours it into a glass rimmed with sugar and salt, and adds his special touch, a float of red wine.

"Bam!" he says as he serves it.

Emily takes a sip. "Man oh man, that's nice," she says.

"Told you."

"*My* secret is Squirt."

"I know a girl that makes them that way. She says it's how they do it in Mexico."

"It's actually called a paloma."

Joe keeps the conversation going while filling orders. He lets Emily do most of the talking. She's thirty-six, was born in Brentwood, and went to college at UCLA, went to college in San Francisco, went to college in New York.

"What did you study?" Joe asks her.

"Art, psychology, dance," she replies. "I finally got a degree in film."

"You gonna make a movie?"

"I've *made* movies, darling. Just nothing anybody wants to see."

"I want to see them," Joe says.

"Most recently I was living in Chicago, working at a gallery," Emily says. "It closed, so now I'm out here mooching off my sister until I figure out what to do next."

"That's cool," Joe says. "That house is a pretty sweet place to crash."

"What about you?" Emily says.

"What about me?" Joe says.

"Did you go to college?"

"I went into the Marines, got a different kind of education."

"I believe that, you know, no joke," Emily says. "I've learned more bartending than I ever did at school."

"Me too," Joe says. "I'm a goddamn genius."

Shannon orders another round for the VIP room. Some dude starts talking to Emily while Joe's making the drinks, explaining something that happened in the game, which is showing on the TV above the jukebox. A tinge of possessiveness tightens a muscle in the back of Joe's neck. As soon as he finishes the order, letting Baba deliver it this time, he interrupts Mr. Baseball's lesson on bunting to ask Emily if she's seen the bar's photo booth.

"I have not," she says.

He takes her into the back room where the pool table and arcade games are. There's also a vintage photo booth. Pulling aside its curtain, he motions her inside.

"You too," she says.

The stool's too small for both of them, so she sits on Joe's lap. He feeds bills into the slot and leans back. Her head is next to his. Their cheeks brush, and he doesn't have to fake a smile when the get-ready light goes on. They look into the camera for the first shots, but after the second flash, Emily turns and Joe feels her lips on his ear. He turns toward her for the next shot, and they kiss, barely, jokingly.

"Accident!" Emily says. "Total accident!"

"You taste good!" Joe says.

While they wait for the photos to develop, Emily appraises the customers shooting pool and playing Asteroids and Ms. Pac-Man. "Looks like a mellow crowd," she says.

"It's rich hipster kids mostly," Joe says. "But every once in a while things get crazy. I've had a couple knives pulled on me."

"How exciting," Emily says, poking fun at his nonchalance.

"You've heard the famous story, haven't you?" Joe asks her.

"What famous story?" Emily says.

"Back when this place was a hangout for cops, some knucklehead came in and tried to rob it by pretending a comb was a pistol. A cop sitting at the bar shot him dead, and for years afterward they had a sign up that said, *Use a Comb, Go to Heaven*."

The photos drop into the tray. Emily snatches up the strip and examines it. Her smile fades, and she suddenly and viciously tears the strip to pieces.

"What's up?" Joe says.

"I look like a monster," Emily says, dropping the pieces to the floor and scattering them with her foot.

Joe reaches into his pocket for more money. "We'll try again."

"No," Emily says. "I've got to go."

Joe follows her back through the bar, calling out to Baba that he's going on break. He's right behind Emily when she walks out the door.

"Hold on a second," he says.

She ignores him, keeps hurrying away.

"Did I say something wrong?" he calls after her. "If so, I'm sorry."

She jerks to a stop and turns to face him. Tears shine in her eyes. Joe lights a cigarette.

"Can I have one of those?" she says.

He lets her pull her own from the pack and hands her his lighter. She takes a deep drag and holds it in.

"I shouldn't have come," she says. "I'm a mess."

Joe points to a woman on the corner selling food off a grill. "Want a hot dog?" he says.

"Sure," Emily says. "A hot dog sounds great."

Joe orders two bacon-wrapped dogs with everything— grilled onions, ketchup, mayonnaise. He and Emily sit on the curb to eat them.

"You're not married, are you?" Emily asks, like maybe that's something he's been keeping from her.

"I was, for a few months a long time ago," he says.

"No kids?"

"No kids," he says. "Are you? Married?"

"For six years," Emily says. "We split up two years ago."

"Kids?" Joe says.

Emily shows him a photo on her phone of a little girl. "Her name's Phoebe," she says. "She's eight. My life blew up after the divorce, and my husband ended up with custody."

"Blew up how?" Joe says.

"He left me for my best friend, and I didn't handle the situation very well. Then he got a job in Austin, and I got tired of fighting and let him move Phoebe there. We FaceTime and stuff, but it's not the same. She's growing up so fast."

"When did you last see her in person?"

Emily tears up again, traffic lights bobbing in her eyes. "Six months ago," she says. "As soon as I get settled here, though, I'm petitioning for more rights."

"That's good," Joe says. "You should."

"It's fucking rough, man," Emily says. Joe can see she's having trouble holding herself together. He changes the subject.

"How old did you say she was?" he asks.

"She's eight," Emily says.

"When *I* was eight, me and my friends invented our own money. We scrounged empty soda cans, flattened them, and used them to buy stuff off each other. I used thirty-six A&W root beers to buy a Game Boy from Pete Brydon, but his mom made me give it back."

Two Harleys drive by, their engines popping like machine guns. Joe's stomach clenches—Iraq—and Emily puts her hands over her ears.

"I don't remember much about my childhood," she says. "It was pretty boring."

"I was scared shitless most of the time," Joe says. "When you're scared, things stick."

"I believe they call that trauma," Emily says, still sad, but grinning a little.

"Sounds about right," Joe says. "I was raised by maniacs."

"'They fuck you up, your mum and dad. They may not mean to, but they do,'" Emily says.

"What's that, a poem?"

"It is. By Philip Larkin."

" 'There's a race of men that don't fit in, a race that can't stay still,' " Joe recites, " 'so they break the hearts of kith and kin, and they roam the world at will.' "

"Is that about you?" Emily says.

"Nah," Joe says. "I've never been anywhere. Anywhere cool anyway."

Emily stands and tosses her napkin into a trash can. "Thanks for the hot dog. You're a good guy," she says.

Joe wants to give her his number, tell her to call if she needs someone to talk to, but he's afraid of spooking her. Instead he says, "Let your sister know I'll be up to fix that fence on Saturday."

"Saturday. Okay," Emily says.

They start out shaking hands but end up in a hug. Joe offers to walk her to her car.

"That's okay," she says. "Get back to work."

Joe hurries to the bar. The DJ is setting up. Kool and the Gang blares, and flecks of light from the disco ball spinning on the ceiling glide across the dance floor and climb the walls. As soon as the game's over the place will fill up again and stay crowded until closing.

Joe goes back to the photo booth and picks up the pieces of the strip of pictures. The top photo is only torn a little. Emily doesn't look like a monster in it, she looks great. He brushes a bit of dirt off the picture and slips it into his wallet.

July 31, 1:15 a.m.

"Gaily bedight,
A gallant knight,
In sunshine and in shadow,
Had journeyed long,
Singing a song,
In search of Eldorado."
What the fuck is that?
One thing I did in prison was memorize poems.
Is this a joke?
It was exercise for my brain.
And you still remember them?
"If you can talk with crowds and keep your virtue,
Or walk with Kings — nor lose the common touch,
If neither foes nor loving friends can hurt you,
If all men count with you, but none too much;
If you can fill the unforgiving minute
With sixty seconds' worth of distance run,
Yours is the Earth and everything that's in it,
And — which is more — you'll be a Man, my son!"

6: TIGER, LEBRON, AND BIGGIE

SATURDAY MORNING JOE GOES DOWN TO THE KITCHEN TO heat a can of chili and scramble some eggs for breakfast. As soon as he sets his plate on the big table in the dining room, Leland comes barreling in like he's been lying in wait. A tall, skinny Black man with a patchy afro and thick glasses, he lives in the house's attic.

"Can I show you something interesting?" he says, and sits without waiting for an answer, one of his notebooks already open. He never goes anywhere without a stack of battered spiral-bound notebooks. He's deep into numerology, and the books are filled with his calculations, page after page of densely packed, neatly printed equations that he believes explain every-thing from the high price of gas to why the Clippers keep losing.

He's eager to pass on this knowledge, but all Joe hears when he's unlucky enough to be cornered by him are streams of numbers and high-intensity blather that makes no more sense than the ravings of a bus-bench psycho. This morning's rant is about a link between Tiger Woods, LeBron James, and Biggie Smalls.

"Tiger and LeBron were born on the same day, December thirtieth, Tiger in 1975 and LeBron in 'eighty-four. So, see here, LeBron: one plus two plus three plus zero plus one plus nine plus eight plus four equals twenty-eight. Two plus eight equals ten. One plus zero equals one. Now, Tiger: one plus two plus three plus zero..."

Joe stares at the wallpaper, pink flowers on a pale green background, and wonders if it's original, wonders how something so fragile could have lasted so long. He checks his phone. Leland doesn't care; he keeps right on talking. There's a text from Shannon confirming another shift at the bar tonight.

"Tiger won his first big tournament when he was twenty-one, okay?" Leland says. "And Biggie was born on May twenty-first, 1972. It's nine thousand, nine hundred and three days from then to when Tiger won, and nine nine zero three equals twenty-one!"

"You lost me," Joe says, gathering his dishes.

"Hold on, hold on," Leland says.

"I've got to go to work."

Joe's head is pounding. He closed the Lotus Lounge last night. It's beer and wine only there, but Nita was pouring shots of happy water, the Thai moonshine she keeps in a Gatorade bottle under the bar, and that led to a sad twenty-dollar hand job out back by the dumpster. Thinking about it this morning disgusts him, so he doesn't think about it.

He scrounges a saw, a hammer, and a box of nails from the

shed in the backyard and calls Uber. His driver, from Haiti, is a real go-getter. When he's not using his car, he rents it to other drivers, and he also owns a janitorial service with four employees: himself, his wife, his daughter, and his brother. He says he prays God blesses Joe like he's been blessed and gives him some business cards in case he meets anyone who needs an office cleaned.

Emily's sister's son answers the door at the sister's house. The kid's wearing a furry hat with cat ears. Joe tells him he's there to work on the fence.

"Okay?" the kid says, like Joe was stupid for knocking.

"Just letting you know," Joe says.

He walks down the side of the house to the backyard. He waited until today to do the job because he figured there'd be less chance of running into Keith, and it seems he was right. There's also no sign of Emily as he passes by the guesthouse.

The lumber is where he stashed it. He nails a couple of one-by-sixes to the existing fence so that they extend three feet above it and cuts more to put up horizontally between them. No way a coyote's getting over that. The rusty saw is screechingly dull, but he makes it work. The more he sweats, the better he feels, as last night's poison leaches out of him. A small, white butterfly lights on his arm, and he shoos it away, worried it'll keel over if it tongues his skin.

Emily sneaks up on him as he's driving the last nail. In spite of the other night's weirdness, he was hoping to see her.

"Looks good," she says about the fence.

"It's solid, at least," he replies. The sky has a funny smear across it, a greasy rainbow. Not pretty, disturbing. He gathers his tools and asks Emily if he can steal a drink from the garden hose.

"I've got good water in my fridge," she says.

He waits outside the guesthouse while she fetches a bottle of Mountain Valley. After gulping half of it, he says, "How are things going?"

"I'm settling into a routine," Emily says. "But I don't know if that's good or bad."

"Depends on the routine, I guess."

"I was wondering if you'd show up today."

"Why?"

"I thought I'd scared you off."

"Were you trying to?"

Emily shrugs. "I don't know," she says. "Maybe."

"You had a bad night," Joe says. "I have them too."

Emily concentrates on one of her fingers, tugs at a hangnail. "Living here's strange," she says. "It's like I've moved back in with my parents. I thought I was handling it pretty well, but maybe I'm fooling myself."

"Don't freak out over nothing," Joe says. "You're getting adjusted."

"Hello?" Emily's sister steps through the slider onto the patio with a frown on her face.

Emily stiffens, making Joe feel like they've been caught doing something they're not supposed to. "I'm all finished," he says to the sister, and quickly takes her over to show her the work. She barely looks at the fence, though, and acts like she's in a hurry to get rid of him.

"How much do I owe you?" she says.

"A hundred and twenty total," Joe says. "Do you want the receipt for the lumber?"

"No, that's fine," she says. "Is a check okay?"

"Sure," Joe says, and waits on the patio while she walks inside to get it. Emily's sitting with her feet in the pool.

"I'm going to the beach tomorrow," she says quietly, so her sister won't hear. "Do you want to come with me?"

"I don't have a car," Joe says.

"I'll drive. Give me your number."

She types it into her phone, then stands and shakes the water off her legs. "Be ready around eleven," she says, heading for the guesthouse.

Her sister brings the check. "I'll walk you out," she says, and leads him along the side of the house. He feels her eyes on his back all the way down the driveway.

With no home game, early evening is mellow at the Short Stop, the jukebox down low, the air-conditioning up high. The door opens briefly, flooding the room with sunlight, and Mitchell, a happy-hour regular, slips inside and makes his way to the bar. He shows up at six every day when there's not a game and leaves as soon as the DJ starts and the younger crowd shows up. He's originally from Boston and wears one of those hats guys from Boston wear. Joe called it a newsboy cap once, and he flipped out.

"It's not a newsboy cap, it's a fucking scally!"

Tonight he's bitching about the heat when Joe sets his beer-and-shot special in front of him.

"My porcelain Irish skin can't take this sun," he says, wiping sweat off his forehead with his napkin. "I got burnt walking from my car." He's around Joe's age, moved to L.A. twenty years ago and works on a TV cooking show. Ninety-nine percent of his conversations revolve around how everything— music, sports, movies—sucks these days compared to when he was a kid. Joe plays along but doesn't actually give a damn if the song on the jukebox is a White Stripes rip-off. Talking to the guy reminds him of being in Chino, of shooting the shit just to kill time.

Baba's flirting with a pair of Mexican girls from the neighborhood. Hipsters, not *cholitas*. They're sitting where Emily sat the other night. Joe scoffs at himself for noticing. He swore he wasn't going to drink this evening in order to be in good shape for the beach tomorrow, but he's in a shitty mood, so he tosses back a shot of Jack. Instead of making him feel better, the booze tilts him further toward darkness, a dangerous place to be at the beginning of a long night.

Some dude snaps his fingers near his face like he's waking him from a trance and says, "Hey, Pops."

"What did you call me?" Joe says.

The dude grins at the buddy beside him, like *Check out the tough guy,* and says, "Just trying to get a drink, bro."

Joe steps to the shitbird, rests his forearms on the bar so he's eye-to-bulging-eye with him, the maddest dog ever at the end of its chain, and leaves the next thing to happen up to him. A Ramones song comes on the juke, one of the Mexican girls pretends to slap Baba, and Shannon walks in, yakking on her phone.

"Two draft PBRs, please," the dude says, backing down.

Joe takes a deep breath, resets, and goes to draw the beers.

"Get yourself one too," the dude says.

"No thanks," Joe says.

A cigarette and another shot set him close to right, and the gummy Mitchell hands him before he splits is the cherry on top. By the time the Saturday-night crowd rolls in, he's half drink-slinging machine, half cosmic cowboy, focused but mellow, and one or two degrees wiser than everyone else in the place.

A girl lets him know someone's puked all over the women's bathroom.

"How is that even possible?" Baba says. "It's barely ten."

"We're all traveling at different speeds," Joe replies, and calls for Manuel. *"Limpia las damas, por favor."*

By one, his high has faded to muzziness. Baba catches him yawning and asks if he wants a bump. Five minutes later he's in the storeroom, bent over a fat line of coke drawn with the Haitian's card.

"I hope that was all for me," he says to Baba when he gets back behind the bar.

"Yeah, yeah, it's cool," Baba says. "I got plenty more."

At last call the kid starts bugging him to come with him to Taco Taco, an after-hours club. "I'll drive and pay your way in, and we can leave whenever you want," he says. After another line and another shot, his fourth or fifth of the night, Joe's too fucked up to fight the current any longer. He winds up in Baba's Honda, speeding toward downtown. And you know what, that's okay. That's fine. Better to be out and about when he's this wired than tossing and turning in his cell at Junior's. As far as the beach tomorrow, even if he doesn't get to bed until four or five, he can still be up by ten. He and Baba do more blow, Joe holding the key under the kid's nose at red lights.

"How much is in these things?" Joe asks when they finish another bindle.

"Ten bucks' worth," Baba says.

"You buy dime bags of coke?"

"That's how my dude sells it."

"You should buy it by the gram or, fuck it, get an eight ball."

"I'm not that hard-core."

"But you're getting ripped off!" Joe realizes he's yelling. He settles back in his seat and counts cars to calm down.

Taco Taco is on Seventh at the foot of the bridge to East

L.A. By day, it's a no-frills café selling food to workers from nearby factories and warehouses. After midnight, if you have twenty dollars and get the nod from the hulking vato gatekeeper, you can enter through the back door and whoop it up till dawn. The vato recognizes Joe and Baba and lets them right in. They've been here before, and white boys stand out.

It takes Joe's eyes a few minutes to adjust to the smoky, skunky murk. It's like being at the bottom of the ocean with all the eels and the crabs. The revelers are mostly Latino—Mexican, Salvadorian, Guatemalan—and mostly male. They bob their heads to the heavy beat of the Spanish-language hip-hop booming out of giant speakers, mouthing the lyrics and throwing up hand signs. The restaurant's counter serves as the bar. Cute girls in booty shorts and bikini tops sell forty-ounce Tecates and plastic shot glasses of tequila.

Joe and Baba grab beers and maneuver through the crowd to a second room, where there's a craps setup, two blackjack tables, and a dozen flashing slot machines. Joe figures out why Baba was so hot to come tonight when he spots the Mexican girls the dude was hitting on earlier at the Shorty. Baba goes off to talk to them, leaving Joe by himself.

He thinks he might play cards, but every seat at both tables is taken. The twenty-five-dollar minimum is too rich for him anyway. He watches a Chinese guy, an older man in a suit and sunglasses, who's betting a hundred bucks a hand. The other, younger players bluster and howl at every turn of the cards, but the Chinese guy sits silent and still, stirring only to rake in his winnings or push out more chips. Joe's digging his style until the dude pulls a cigarette from his pack, taps it on the table, and lights the wrong end.

Joe turns to look for Baba and sees Danny Bones with some of his boys. Danny's a fortyish Boyle Heights gangster who started on corners but leveled up to become a dealer to the stars. Now he knows actors, rappers, Lakers. Joe met him at the Short Stop and has sent more than a few customers his way. He gets the idea he should introduce Baba to him and drags the kid away from the girls, saying, "I got someone I want you to meet."

"But I don't want to meet anybody," Baba says.

Danny stares blankly at them as they approach.

"What's up, chief?" Joe says.

"Joe Hustle," Danny says, still blank. He wears old-school Pendleton and Dickies cholo drag, but all his original garbage tattoos have been covered by custom work by Mr. Cartoon, which is the street equivalent of flashing a Rolex to let fools know what's what.

"This is my buddy, Baba O'Reilly," Joe says. "He works at the Shorty with me."

Danny gives Baba an almost imperceptible whassup nod.

"Baba likes to get down," Joe says, tapping his nose.

"So?" Danny says.

His disdain slices through the fog in Joe's head. A kid like Baba, a gangster like Danny. What the fuck was he thinking? "So remember him," he says, not letting on that he knows he's screwed up.

Danny hisses and smiles a mean smile. "Yeah, okay, I'll remember," he says, and turns to his homies, ending the conversation.

Joe tells Baba he's ready to go. Baba complains they just got there, but Joe reminds him of his promise to leave when Joe wanted. This doesn't sit well with Baba. All the way to Filipi-notown he whines about how Joe ruined his night, and he refuses to drive him up to the house, dumping him on Temple instead. As Joe plods up the hill, a strange sound prompts him to look down. The sidewalk is covered with snails. He turns back to see ten or so crushed to snot in his wake.

He hurries across the porch, through the living room, and up the stairs to his room. Janey has tucked a yellow card between his door and the frame. *Get out of Hell Free,* it reads, and there's a drawing of a little man in prison stripes. Joe recites the prayer on the back of the card, "Dear Lord Jesus, I know that I am a sinner...," but it doesn't make him feel any better.

July 22, 10:12 p.m.

The shit you saw over there must have fucked you up.

Loud noises sometimes, but, nah, I'm good, I'm strong. I knew what I was getting into when I enlisted. I put myself in that situation. I got *paid* to be in that situation.

Did they at least give you a medal?

[Laughter] Yeah, and then took it back. The fight at the bridge was the only action I saw. I was on a base the rest of my time in country. That's where I started drinking again. Alcohol was against regs, but we bought moonshine off the locals, haji juice. We mixed it with lemonade, made Saddam Slammers. I got busted for being lit on guard duty and busted again for beating the shit out of somebody, and when we got back to Lejune they cut me loose with a General Discharge. I went in a drunk and came out a drunk.

They could have offered you some help.

They made me talk to a shrink. I told him what happened at the bridge and said I'd been having nightmares, but all he did was ask if I drank. "Yeah, I drink," I said. "That's your problem," he said. "Stop." They don't want to help you in the service, they just want you to behave.

7: NEVER OR THEN?

The next morning Joe sleeps through Emily's first text—*Still up for the beach?*—and her second—*You there?*—but the chirp at ten thirty finally rouses him. He grabs his phone, reads, *I'm leaving soon,* and replies with *Not without me.* He tells her to pick him up at the McDonald's on Temple and Alvarado.

A quick shower, and last night swirls down the drain like dirt. Two Bud Lights get his juices flowing, and his first cigarette is magic. A McGriddle and a large coffee complete the cure.

Emily pulls into the parking lot in a convertible Mini Cooper Joe saw in the driveway of her sister's house. She's wearing jean shorts, a man's dress shirt, and mirrored aviators.

"Sorry I left you hanging for a while," Joe says as he climbs in. "I worked at the bar last night."

"Get any knives pulled on you?" Emily says.

Joe can't remember the last time he rode in a convertible. When they skirt downtown on the 110, he stretches out both arms as if reaching for the high-rises and wiggles his fingers in the breeze.

"Do you like this car?" he asks Emily.

"It's cute," she says. "It's my niece's."

"Wind in your hair," Joe says. "Sun on your face."

"You sound like a commercial," she says.

She's streaming Steely Dan on the radio: "Hey Nineteen," "Rikki Don't Lose That Number." Joe sings along to "Deacon Blues," to the part about the winners in the world. Working in bars for so many years, he knows a few lines of every song written since 1965.

"My dad used to listen to these guys, and I hated them," Emily says. "Now I think they're incredible."

"Good driving music for sure," Joe says.

They turn north when they hit the coast and head up PCH. The sky's pale blue, the ocean indigo, and the water glitters like it's full of diamonds. Joe glimpses white sand between the houses lining the highway, crashing waves, wheeling gulls.

Emily says the only thing she misses about L.A. when she's away is the beach. "We were down here every day in the summer when I was a kid."

"It was such a hassle to get here from Burbank, me and my buddies only came over once or twice a year," Joe says. "Even after we got cars, that thirty miles was like a hundred."

"So you don't know how to surf?" Emily says.

"You ever tried?" Joe says. "It's hard."

"I'm gonna learn," Emily says. "I saw a video of this surf school in Nicaragua, and I'm going down there and taking lessons."

The parking lot at Topanga's full, so they keep driving.

Most of the time they're quiet, listening to music and taking in the scenery, but it's not like separate individuals lost in their own thoughts, alone even while together. It's like two people sharing something so nice and feeling so much the same about it that there's no fear of silence even though they're still practically strangers.

Every beach in Malibu is packed, and so is Zuma. When they get to El Matador, Emily says, "We can stop here or keep going."

"Drive on," Joe says.

She changes the music to Snoop Dogg's *Doggystyle,* and Joe makes her laugh by rapping about kicking a little sumthin' for the Gs. He tells her about the time he did "Who Am I?" for his junior high talent show. Ten minutes later they luck into a spot above a short stretch of beach just past the county line. There are houses at both ends of the crescent of sand, but besides that it's ocean, sky, and rocks, and the breaking of the waves drowns out the noise from the highway.

They spread the blanket Emily brought on an open patch of sand between a family with a toddler and a deeply tanned couple glistening with oil. Joe strips to his bathing suit and watches from the corner of his eye as Emily steps out of her shorts and unbuttons her shirt to reveal a black bikini and a body that's everything he's been imagining it would be. She knows he's peeking, he's sure of it, but she doesn't seem to mind. Nonetheless he pretends to focus on a flock of pelicans diving out beyond the breakers while she spreads sunscreen over her legs, her arms, her stomach.

"Do my back," she says.

Joe kneels behind her and smears the cream on her neck and shoulders. The first time he got laid was on a chaise lounge on the pool deck of an older girl who lived down the street.

Summer vacation, fourteen years old, stoned on weed the chick had swiped from her parents. The smell of sunscreen always brings it back.

"I'm getting in the water," he says. "Want to come?"

"Let me get some sun first," Emily says.

Joe jogs out until he's up to his knees, then slows to a walk. The water's warm where it's shallow but gets colder the deeper he goes. He forges on, gritting his teeth, as first his balls are chilled, then his belly, then his chest.

The waves are breaking higher than his head at the surf line. He bounces in the swell and waits for the next set to roll in. Something brushing his leg spooks him. The water's too murky to see what it is. He dog-paddles to a new spot a dozen feet away.

He's watching a group of surfers to the south and doesn't notice a big wave bearing down on him. When he feels the suck signaling it's about to break, it's too late to dive under. The wave swallows him like a whale, swirls him in its mouth, and spits him out, leaving him wobbly but exhilarated.

He palms salt water out of his eyes and sets up, watching over his shoulder as the next wave barrels toward him. He begins to kick and stroke at exactly the right moment, and the wave scoops him up and carries him shoreward. It's the longest, fastest ride he's ever had, and he roars at the top of his lungs as he zips along the face.

When the wave finally fizzles, he wades out to catch another, but no such luck. He starts swimming either too early or too late, or the waves don't have enough power to carry him. After fifteen minutes of flailing, he gives up and heads in.

He's almost to shore, high-stepping in three feet of water, when something jabs his left ankle. He jumps and yelps and dashes the last ten yards to dry sand. A trickle of bright red blood oozes from a tiny puncture above his heel, a tiny puncture that hurts like hell.

"Stingray got you," says a passing beach bum. He crouches beside Joe and probes the wound with his finger. "There's no barb, so you're cool. Piss on it to kill the pain for now and soak it in hot water when you get home."

Joe limps to the blanket. Emily, lying on her back, propped on her elbows, grimaces when she sees the blood.

"Oh my God!"

"I stepped on a stingray," Joe says.

"What do we do?"

"That guy said to piss on it."

Emily squints, skeptical. "Seriously?" she says.

"I can't reach. Can you do it?"

"Pee on you?"

"It's burning like fire," Joe says. "We'll go down by the water. Nobody'll notice."

They walk until they come to wet sand and seaweed. Emily lifts Joe's foot to her crotch. "Don't watch," she says. Joe turns away, and a second later hot urine gushes onto the wound. The pain fades immediately.

"You picked a pretty elaborate way to get a golden shower," Emily says.

Joe, balancing on one foot, laughs so hard, he falls over.

Emily wades out up to her waist to rinse off.

"Keep going!" Joe shouts.

"Hell, no," she screeches. "I'm not giving you an excuse to piss on *me*!"

They return to the blanket. Emily digs a Band-Aid out of her bag and places it over the puncture. The skin surrounding it is red and swollen.

"Yuck," Emily says.

"It's fine," Joe replies.

They lie back and let the sun dry them. Emily takes out her copy of *Anna Karenina*. Joe asks her to read to him. She hems and haws but eventually gives in. The man in the book is in love with a girl. He once asked her to marry him, but she said no. Years later they're playing a game where he writes the first letters of the words of a sentence, and she tries to guess the sentence. The letters he writes are w, y, a, m, t, c, b, d, i, m, n, o, and t, and the girl figures out he's asking "When you answered me, 'That can't be,' did it mean never or then?"

"No way she got that!" Joe exclaims. Emily shushes him and goes on. The girl answers the man in the same way, writing that she couldn't give him any other answer back then. "And now?" the man says. The scene ends with him asking her again to marry him and her saying yes this time.

"And they all lived happily ever after," Joe says.

"Not everybody," Emily says. "I already know how the book ends."

The tanned couple next door can't keep their hands off each other. Joe spies on them through his eyelashes. The guy massages the girl's ass with his hairy, big-knuckled tarantula hand, and she circles one of his nipples with a purple fingernail. The dude reminds Joe of the porn freak who rents the room next to his.

The sun's heat is tempered by a cool breeze that makes Joe feel like he's wrapped in velvet. He empties his head and focuses on his breathing. It's a relaxation technique a prison shrink taught him. He times his breaths to the crashing of the waves, and two minutes later he's out, half dreaming he's the one groping the girl with the purple fingernails. He's a little embarrassed when Emily rouses him to ask if he's ready for lunch.

★ ★ ★

They cross the freeway to a busy seafood shack on the other side. Joe's limping some, but the foot only really hurts when he tries to run. Twenty or so motorcycles rumble into the parking lot. They're not real bikers, Vagos or Mongols. They're weekend warriors who put on leather jackets and boots and meet up on Sundays to tool around on their expensive toys — big tippers when they sometimes roll into the Short Stop.

Joe pays for his fish and chips, Emily's boiled shrimp, and a pitcher of beer while Emily snags a spot on the patio. The food's pricey for a joint with picnic tables, porta potties, and no waitstaff. There isn't enough on Joe's debit card to cover it, so he hands the cashier three twenties.

Maneuvering through the crowd with the pitcher, he spots Emily waving from a table. "I feel like I'm working at the bar," he says as he settles onto the bench across from her. He's dying for a beer and quickly fills their mugs.

"I love this place," Emily says. "I used to come all the time when I lived out here."

"When was that?"

"While I was married. We lived in Malibu in a mobile home my ex's parents owned."

"That must have been cool," Joe says. "Movie stars and stuff."

Emily waves this away. "Movie stars don't impress me," she says. "I grew up in Brentwood, and everyone there was a movie star or a movie star's kid."

"There was this family on my street, the Waynes," Joe says. "The mom got her kids agents and took them to auditions all the time. The boy, Brian, was in a commercial for Libby's peas, and his mom bought a BMW with the money he made off it. My mom saw that and was like, 'Do you think you'd like to act?' and I was like, 'There's no fucking way. I'm never, I don't care how much they pay me, dressing like a cowboy and singing about peas.'"

He doesn't tell her the rest of the story, that Brian shot himself the week he turned fourteen.

"I went through the whole acting thing in high school," Emily says. "My parents weren't into it at all. With them, it was doctor or lawyer, that's it."

"So you gave it up?" Joe says.

"I figured out pretty quickly on my own that I sucked, so, luckily, I didn't waste too much time on it."

Joe picks up the food when their number's called. His fish is perfect, nice and crispy. Emily goes to work on her shrimp, peeling them and dunking them in cocktail sauce. The crowd's lively, people taking pictures of each other, people telling jokes. A squeal of brakes from the highway makes everyone pause for a second and look over, but it's nothing, a close call.

Joe tosses a fry to a one-legged gull in the parking lot and asks Emily, "Have you decided what's next?"

"What do you mean?" Emily says.

"You said the other night you were staying with your sister until you decided what to do next."

"Did I?" Emily says. She sounds perturbed.

"I'm not trying to be nosy," Joe says.

Emily continues like she didn't hear him. "My mother thinks I should get a real estate license," she says. "My dad's all about nursing school, and my sister is sure I could get into law school somewhere. Do you want to tell me what *you* think I should do?"

"I think you should do whatever makes you happy," Joe says.

"Whatever makes me happy," Emily says with a scowl. "Great."

"Truthfully?" Joe says. "I don't give a fuck what you do."

"Nor should you," Emily says. "So can I ask you a favor? Don't ever give me advice. I get all the advice I can stand from everyone else in my life. Just be my friend."

"Okay, friend," Joe says. "Let's have some more beer." He picks up the pitcher and refills their mugs.

Emily exhales through pursed lips and fans her face with her hand. "Man," she says. "I am such a freak."

"No, you're not," Joe says.

"'Do what makes you happy,'" she says. "Everybody always says that. Are you happy?"

Joe sips his beer and shrugs. "Today I am," he says.

When they return to the beach, the couple with the baby is gone, and so are the gropers. Emily opens her book, and Joe lies back and watches the surfers. He dozes off again and dreams he's working at Wahid's liquor store. All kinds of crazy shit happens: a robbery, an earthquake, a fire. It's too much dream for such a short nap, and he wakes confused about what's real and what's not. He runs out into the water, risking another sting to bring himself fully back to the world.

A fog bank forms offshore and sucks up all the heat. People take down their umbrellas, grab their coolers, and trudge to their cars. Emily's reluctant to leave, keeps saying, "A little longer." Joe slips his arm around her, she rests her head on his shoulder, and they sit side by side wrapped in the blanket until the fog snuffs out the sun. It's the longest Joe's been that close to anyone in years.

They continue up PCH to Oxnard and cut over to the 101 to get back to L.A. Emily tells Joe about a film she made in college, a documentary about a homeless guy who played guitar for tips on Fisherman's Wharf. One night the dude got tweaked on angel dust and beat her up, but she went back the next day and kept shooting. "He was schizophrenic, but very gentle, very kind when he wasn't tripping," she says. "The shitty thing is, I only got a C on the project."

"Did you put in the stuff about him attacking you?" Joe says.

"I didn't," Emily says. "And that's why the film didn't work. It was a lie."

Joe's embarrassed for her to see Junior's house, but she might as well know where he stands in the world. The place looks especially dilapidated when they pull up in front, like an abandoned building occupied by squatters. Robert and Candy are playing badminton in the yard.

"I've lived in houses like this," Emily says.

"No, you haven't," Joe says. "But now that I'm back at the bar, I'll be getting my own joint soon." ·

"Can I visit you there?" Emily says.

"Anytime," Joe says.

When he leans in, she's there to meet him. The kiss is a long one. They break off for a second to look into each other's eyes and go right into another. Joe caresses one of her tits through her shirt. She gently pushes him away.

"We're not gonna fuck in my niece's car," she says.

"The house is a pigsty," Joe says.

"We're not fucking at all. Not tonight. I'm not ready."

"Me, neither," Joe says.

Emily smiles at the joke and lets that be the end of it.

Joe feels fine when she drives off, not frustrated, not disappointed. If something happens, it happens. He's never been the kind of guy to push things.

It's a thousand degrees inside the house and stinks like rotting bananas. His foot hurts going up the stairs to his room, and when he pulls off his shoe, he finds that the wound has bled through the Band-Aid. He limps to the bathroom, fills the tub with hot water, and soaks his foot until the water turns pink. After he dabs Neosporin on the puncture and rigs a better bandage out of a sock and duct tape, it's beer time.

He was going to see if Matt would let him take the Prius out but decides to kick it instead. He pitches in with Junior, Robert, and Candy for pizza, and they watch *Lord of the Rings* on the living room TV. He's nodding on the couch, stoned from a bomber Junior passed around, when a text comes from Emily. *You're hot*, it says. *You're hot too*, he texts back.

July 12, 11:52 p.m.

Tell me this: What killed the dinosaurs?

An asteroid.

How?

An asteroid hit Earth and kicked up a cloud of dust that blocked the sun. Plants couldn't grow, so the dinosaurs that ate plants died, which meant that the dinosaurs that ate those dinosaurs died too.

Nice try, but no. You ever heard of the Expanding Earth theory?

It was an asteroid, bro.

The Expanding Earth theory says that Earth has been expanding ever since it formed. It was a third smaller in dinosaur times, so gravity was weaker. That's why dinosaurs grew so big. As the planet expanded, though, gravity got stronger, and their bones weren't able to support them anymore. They couldn't move, they couldn't hunt, so they died.

Where did you get that?

There's a whole book about it.

There's a whole book about Dracula. Do you believe in Dracula?

This is science, not a story. Do you hear that?

[Pause]

That girl screaming?

Someone's beating the shit out of her.

Don't open the window, man. I have to live here.

Hey! Let her go, motherfucker. I'm calling the cops. Let her go right now.

8: CAN'T HURT STEEL

Joe's mother lives in Las Vegas with her third husband, Frank. When they got married, they sold the Burbank house Joe grew up in and bought a place in Summerlin. She's a dealer and Frank's a bartender at the Gold Coast Casino. Three years ago they invited Joe out for Christmas dinner. He and his mom were at each other's throats before the turkey hit the table, and he ended up brawling with Frank's sons—both sheriffs—and getting thrown out of the house, whereupon he lost five hundred bucks playing rage-fueled blackjack at some North Vegas shitpit. He and his mom haven't talked much since—the last time was six months ago—but today's her birthday, so he gives her a call.

The first thing she asks is, "Are you working?"

"Bartending again," Joe says.

"Where are you living?"

"Echo Park."

"Jesus, don't get shot."

"Houses are a million dollars in Echo Park now," Joe says. "It's a nice place."

"There's no such thing as a nice place in L.A. anymore," his mom says. "You should move here. There are plenty of bartending jobs. We'll help you out."

Frank must be sitting there listening. She has him convinced she's a paragon of motherhood. He's never heard how after Joe's dad got killed, she used to leave Joe alone for days while she went off with this man and that, or how she once beat him with a coat hanger and then kept him out of school until the welts healed. She's been rewriting history for years, knowing it's Joe's word against hers.

Joe lets her go on about golf—when did she start playing golf?—and the Alaska cruise she and Frank booked and how great Frank's kids are doing. When he can't take any more, he tells her he's got to get ready for work. After he hangs up, he stretches out on his bed until he gets his breathing under control. "Can't hurt steel," he chants softly. "Can't hurt steel."

He's in the kitchen, filling his cooler with ice, when Junior comes in. "The water heater's not working," Junior says. "Do you know anything about them?"

"Not much," Joe says.

"I'll give you a free week if you can fix it."

"I'll take a look."

The water heater is strapped to the wall of a stuffy little storage room under the house, a cave filled with cans of dried paint and rusty garden tools. Cobwebs as intricate as lace stretch between the floor joists overhead. The heater's pilot is out. Joe tries to light it, but the flame disappears as soon as he lifts his thumb off the button that gives it gas.

He does some Googling and learns the problem is most likely that the thermocouple has worn out. A new one will only cost eight dollars and take about five minutes to install. Junior lets him use his Jeep to pick up the part at Home Depot. Robert and Candy ride along because they want food from the Panda Express next to the store. They sit in the back seat, pretending Joe's their chauffeur. Robert's wearing a glittery cardboard tiara, and Candy has drawn hearts on her cheeks in red lipstick.

"Have you ever been to an orgy?" she asks Joe.

"Depends what you call an orgy," he says.

"You know, a bunch of people all fucking and sucking and shit."

"How many people?"

"At least six."

"Then, no, I haven't been to an orgy," Joe says.

"We should have one at the house," Candy says.

"That'd be more of a gang bang, considering you'd be the only female," Robert says.

"What about Janey?" Candy says.

"Janey?" Robert says. "That's hot. She'd be all, 'Fuck me! Fuck me! Thank you, Jesus! Hallelujah!'"

"Hallelujah!" Candy yells. "Hallelujah!"

The couple walk to the restaurant while Joe goes into the store. He takes his time, enjoying the air-conditioning and perusing the power drivers, circular saws, and nail guns. One of his goals is to own his own tools again. Every time he manages to collect any, he ends up having to pawn them.

Back at the house, he returns to the storage room to replace the coupler. The job is so simple, he doesn't even need the instructions. When he gets the part screwed in, he sparks the pilot and the heater ignites with a whoosh. He's proud of himself as he emerges into the sunlight, getting it right the first time.

Robert and Candy are eating their orange chicken on the front porch. Junior is out there with them, drinking a beer. Joe tells him there should be plenty of hot water in an hour and goes inside to fry up a can of corned-beef hash.

What makes hash is the egg you poach to go with it, and Joe considers himself a master egg poacher. His secret is swirling the simmering water and adding vinegar to it before sliding in the egg. You need plenty of ketchup, too, to top the finished dish.

Leland catches him in the dining room and launches into a lecture about Malcolm X and the number nineteen. "His booking number was two two eight four three. What's that add up to?" The dude's so skinny, you can see the bones in his shoulders shifting beneath his T-shirt. He lives on granola bars and Gatorade like an astronaut up there in the attic, floating high above Earth with his head full of numbers. Joe considers sharing the hash with him but doesn't. Once you feed a stray, you never get rid of it.

He's having a smoke on the porch when he gets a call from a number he doesn't recognize. Thinking for some reason it might be Emily, he answers. It's not Emily, it's Keith.

"I need your help," Keith says. "I've got to make this quick because I'm using a nurse's phone."

"What's up?" Joe says.

"I fucking OD'd last night and ended up in the hospital. They're moving me to jail soon, and I don't know when I'll bail out. I need you to pick up my truck and keep it for me until I do."

"Why me?" Joe says. He's still angry about the asshole cutting him loose when he wouldn't help him score. "Why not your wife or your brother?"

"If my wife finds out, I'm fucked," Keith says. "She'll leave me, and I'll never see the kids again. And Rodney will tell my parents. I can't deal with that either. I'm begging you, bro. I'll give you a thousand bucks as soon as I'm out."

The money doesn't have any bearing on Joe's decision. Not much, anyway. It's the principle. It's against the law, the real law, to kick a man when he's as down as Keith is now.

"I got you," he says. "Everything's gonna be okay."

Keith overdosed in an Applebee's in Alhambra. After copping out there, he stopped at the restaurant to fix in the bathroom. A ten-year-old boy found him unconscious on the floor of a stall. His F-150 is in the parking lot. Joe has his Uber driver drop him off next to it.

When the original lock on the toolbox in the bed of the truck was punched out a while back, Keith had two hasps welded to the box. Heavy-duty padlocks secure them over two steel loops. Joe dials in the combinations Keith gave him and opens the box. The spare fob is hidden in a canvas glove.

Joe starts the engine and lowers the windows. The dash is so hot, it's soft to the touch, and the air smells like melting plastic. Joe worries the police are watching the truck, waiting to see who comes for it. He checks the rearview mirror every few seconds until he's on the freeway. Sweat slithers down his neck. Turning the air conditioner up high, he aims all the vents his way. He doesn't go any faster than sixty on the drive back to L.A.

After parking around the corner from Junior's to avoid questions about the truck from his housemates, he makes sure nobody's on the street and flips down the sun visor above his head. A Ziploc bag containing half an ounce of China white drops into his lap. "Get rid of it," Keith ordered during the phone call. Next, he opens the glove compartment, and there, right where Keith said it would be, is a nine-millimeter Glock.

He's fizzing with dread as he walks to the house, the gun in his waistband, the dope in his pocket. He's a felon in possession of heroin and a firearm, a fucking idiot with a one-way ticket back to prison. A squirrel chattering at the top of a palm tree nearly stops his heart, and he feels eyes on him everywhere. He goes straight into the backyard and stashes the pistol and the dope in the shed, at the bottom of a box containing a stack of Styrofoam tombstones and a plastic skeleton, Halloween decorations.

His foot's throbbing. He goes up to his room and takes off the bandage. The puncture is more inflamed than ever and tender at its edges. He puts more Neosporin on it. He's lying on the bed with the fan going full blast and staring out the window at the patch of pink stucco next door when Emily texts.

You busy?

Just chilling

Call me

He sits up, clears his throat, and says "Hey" a couple of times, testing his voice. Emily answers on the first ring.

"How's your foot?" she asks.

"It's still there," he says.

"I'm thinking about going to a movie tonight. Want to come?"

"I'm working, but I'm free tomorrow."

"Maybe I'll wait then."

"Dinner's on me if you do."

"Damn, you're really after my ass, aren't you?"

Joe settles back onto his bed after the call, hoping to grab a nap before his shift at the bar. It's only four thirty, but he feels like he's lived three days already. A chorus of moans and groans begins in the room next to his. He pounds on the wall, but nothing happens. "Oh, fuck! Oh, fuck!" some porn star wails. Charging out into the hall, he hammers on the room's door and yells, "Turn that shit down!"

The door flies open, and the Brazilian, Paulo, is standing there in red bikini underpants. He's a big dude, cut like a bodybuilder. He works out with dumbbells in the yard and claims to be an MMA fighter. Candy calls him Conan because of his long dark hair. His eyes are bloodshot, and he's unsteady on his feet, fucked up on something. Joe balls his fists, ready to take him out with a punch to the throat, and says, "You didn't hear me banging on the fucking wall?"

"I don't know you," Paulo slurs in his thick accent. "I don't know what you're trying to do."

"I'm trying to sleep," Joe says. "I've got to work tonight."

"What are you telling me?"

"Don't you have earbuds?"

"I'm not rich, okay? *Desculpa.* I'm poor."

Joe's not sure he's getting through to him. He points to the phone in the guy's hand. "Turn that down," he says. "Turn your phone down."

Paulo brings the phone up so Joe can see people fucking on the screen. He lowers the volume with four or five exaggerated stabs of his thumb.

"Okay, cop?" he says. "Okay, Grandma?"

July 25, 11:31 p.m.

I used to have major game in high school and right after. It was all about fun in those days. Sport fucking. I'm high, you're high, let's get it on! That's how it should be when you're young. Everybody should fuck as many people as they can. The dummies who settle down with the first person they fuck, or the second, or the fifth, always feel like they missed out and end up cheating and shit. It should be a law that—men and women—you have to fuck fifty different people before you get married. You should be bored with getting laid.

You sure were lucky.

How?

All that ass and no kids.

I started lucky, but then I got smart.

What do you mean?

When I was nineteen, I got myself snipped.

You got a vasectomy? Is that even legal when you're nineteen?

The doctor tried to talk me out of it. He said, "Son, I don't think you're mature enough yet to make this decision. You have no idea what your life will be like in five or ten years and what you'll want then," and I was like, "You know what's not gonna change? The fact that my dad was a murderer and my mom is nuts. I'm mature enough to know that someone with sewer water running through his veins shouldn't have children."

So he did it?

I told him if he didn't, I was gonna go to TJ and get it done there.

That's cool and all, but maybe your kids would have beaten the genetic odds.

Maybe, but I'm not a diaper-changer. I'm not a baby-talker. I could never pretend to be into the shit a five-year-old is into.

It's different when you're a dad.

How do you know?

That's what people say, people who have kids.

They're lying.

Have you ever regretted it?

Getting snipped? I don't regret anything.

9: THE TIGERS
COME AT NIGHT

JOE ONLY HAS TWO DRINKS AT WORK AND WAKES UP THE NEXT morning feeling fine. After checking his phone and finding no message from Keith, he tidies his room. He shakes out the sleeping bag he uses as a blanket, brushes off the windowsill ashes from the smokes he sneaks in violation of Junior's no-cigarettes-in-the-house rule, and throws out some beer cans and a pizza box. Laundry is at the top of today's chore list. He strips the sheet off the bed and shoves it into his backpack, along with his dirty T-shirts, underwear, and socks.

The sun starts gnawing on him as soon as he steps off the porch. It's not even noon yet and already a hundred degrees. There's no sense walking to the laundromat when he has Keith's truck. He can't see the F-150 around the corner but hears a beep when he presses the fob. You worry in this kind of neighborhood. He once had a Toyota pickup he named Lupita. Every week something would be missing from it: the battery, the mirrors, the taillights twice. And the trunk lock on his Sentra was punched out so many times, he finally stopped replacing it and used a bungee cord to hold it shut.

The laundromat's air conditioner is on the fritz, and the two swiveling fans they've got going are useless, merely pushing the heat from one corner to another. Joe sticks all his clothes in a single machine and sets it to cold. He adds a box of detergent from the vending machine, then walks outside and stands in the shade with some of the other customers, Mexican and Filipina women yelling into phones and chasing kids.

Feeling thirsty, he buys a bottle of Coke from the 7-Eleven at the other end of the mini-mall. He buys a bag of peanuts, too, and dumps them into the Coke. It's something his dad did, called it Okie breakfast. Some of the nuts sink to the bottom, others float, and the trick is to get a few in every mouthful.

Back at the laundromat, he scores a plastic chair next to the open door. There's a hint of a breeze there, and he can keep an eye on the truck. A shifty little vato with a blunt tucked over one ear nods as he passes by, then suddenly changes course to come inside. "Check it out," he says, showing Joe a lottery ticket. "This here's a winner. Twenty grand." He presents another ticket, a printout of the winning numbers. "See for yourself."

It's the setup for a scam usually pulled on old ladies. Joe can't believe the guy's trying it on him. "Do I look stupid?" he says.

"Seriously, dog," the vato says.

"Get the fuck out of here."

The vato puffs his chest and says, "Fuck you, you fucking

faggot," but backs quickly out the door when Joe jumps to his feet and keeps backing down the walkway until he's certain he's not coming after him.

Next on Joe's list is a haircut. When his clothes are dry, he carries them out to the truck, starts the engine, and turns on the air conditioner. The sun's shining in his eyes. He pulls down the visor and sees a photo stuck there he didn't see before, Keith's wife and kids. He flips the visor back up.

His barber shop is near MacArthur Park. It's changed over the past couple years. The old owner retired and handed the business to his son, who gave the place a retro pinup-and-hot-rod makeover and now courts the rockabilly, wallet-chain crowd. He also raised the price of a haircut by ten bucks. Joe's regular barber, an ancient Cuban, is still there, though, so Joe keeps coming back.

The old man's chair is empty when Joe walks in even though a bunch of guys are waiting for cuts. They prefer the younger barbers, with their tattoos and pompadours. The Cuban recognizes Joe and motions for him to sit. Joe's private nickname for him is Mumbles because everything he says in his sandpaper whisper fades into unintelligibility after a few words. "The Dodgers *mumble mumble*," "The traffic *mumble mumble*."

"Hot out there," he says today, fastening the smock around Joe's neck.

"Hotter than hell," Joe replies.

"The weatherman said *mumble mumble*."

Joe doesn't even try to catch the pronouncement over the buzz of the clippers and the twang of the Chuck Berry album spinning on the vintage record player. He just nods and says, "Huh."

Mumbles is eighty years old. He came over from Havana in 1961 and has lived in the same tiny apartment above a jewelry store on Seventh Street since he got here. That's all Joe knows about him. It's hardly anything, but enough to make them almost friends in L.A. Twenty minutes after Joe hits the chair, the old man whips off the smock and slaps stinging aftershave onto the back of his neck. He shows his dentures in a big smile when Joe tips him five bucks.

Vendors line the sidewalk on Alvarado across from the park. Hawking mangoes and avocados. Hawking sneakers and phone chargers. Hawking used pots and new pans, shampoo and soap, fake IDs and bootleg Viagra. Joe peruses a rack of shirts, thinking he could use a new one to wear tonight. He finds a dark blue button-down in his size and hands over ten dollars. He's once again grateful to be back working at the bar. It feels good to have money in his pocket.

Emily offers him a choice of three movies. He doesn't care which they see but can tell she's used to people having opinions on things like this. "*Spider-Man* sounds good," he says, because it's the only one of the three he's heard of. Keith still hasn't called, so he offers to drive.

"I thought you didn't have a car," Emily says.

"I'm babysitting a friend's truck," he says.

She's supposed to be waiting outside her sister's place at six but is actually down the hill from the house, sitting on the curb and frowning at her phone. Joe doesn't see her until he's passed by but can't back up because there's a car behind him. He pulls into an open driveway to turn around.

"Need a ride?" he calls out the window when he gets back to where she is.

Emily raises a hand to shush him and keeps texting. He puts on the truck's emergency flashers and sits double-parked, waiting for her to finish. She's red-eyed and sniffling when she finally climbs in, has obviously been crying.

"Sorry," she says. "It was my ex."

"Do you want to skip the movie?" Joe asks her.

"Of course not," she says, and leans over to kiss him on the cheek as if it's something they do all the time. "I've got to warn you, though, I've had some wine already."

"I'll catch up," Joe says.

The movie's showing in the Cinerama Dome, where Joe remembers going with his mom when he was a kid. A different actor plays Spider-Man in this film than in the last Spider-Man movie he saw. There's plenty of action, but even so, twenty minutes in, he's fighting to keep his eyes open. He goes in and out during the rest of the film, snapping awake only when something loud happens. Emily kids him about it afterward, and he tells her it was the most expensive nap he ever took.

He suggests Miceli's, an Italian restaurant off Hollywood Boulevard, for dinner, another place his mom used to take him. The restaurant's been there since 1949 and is like something out of a movie, with Chianti bottles hanging from the ceiling, red-and-white checked tablecloths, and singing waiters and waitresses. They order a pizza and a pitcher of beer. A guy in a tux is playing a piano, and their waitress sings a song. Joe doesn't know it, but Emily mouths the words and claps when the girl finishes.

"We did *Les Mis* in high school," she says. "I played Fantine and sang that."

Joe's never heard of *Les Mis* but asks her to sing the song for him.

"Oh, God, you don't want to hear that," she says.

She talks nonstop throughout the meal. About growing up in Brentwood, about dumb things she did in college, about traveling in Europe afterward. She talks so much she barely finishes one slice of pizza. Joe chalks it up to nervousness.

She wants a drink after dinner. They walk to a tourist bar on the Boulevard, wall-to-wall drunks screaming to be heard over booming music and big-screen TVs. Every seat's taken, so they drink their beers standing up.

The noise and the stupid fucking people grate on Joe. He can't tune them out like he does when he's behind the bar. Emily's telling him about something that happened to her in Chicago, but his attention wanders. He watches a girl take a selfie with a hustler in a Freddy Krueger getup. Emily figures out he's not listening when she asks him a question and he doesn't answer.

"Earth to Joe," she says.

"Sorry," he says. "This place is so loud."

"Come on then, let's go."

They share a cigarette on their walk back to the truck. Emily tells him an idea she has for a screenplay. It's a love story between a bank robber and a lady cop, neither of whom knows what the other does when they meet. The cop ends up having to go after the bank robber and shoots him in the end.

"You told that so good, I feel like I already saw it," Joe says when she finishes.

"Telling it's a lot easier than writing it," Emily says.

"That's funny," Joe says, thinking of Matt. "I know a guy who wants to write movies, and he says the same thing."

Joe parks in front of the sister's house. He and Emily make out for a while, grinding and groping and steaming up the truck's windows. Joe's on top of her, a knee between her legs, when she says, "Let's go inside."

"What do you mean?" Joe says.

"You know what I mean."

Joe sits up and stares out the windshield at a tree tossing in the breeze. Its branches and leaves under the streetlight look like a pack of dogs tearing into one another. "I've got to tell you something," he says.

Emily leans against her door, a little flushed, a little sweaty. "You lied about being married," she says.

"I haven't lied about anything," Joe says. "But before we go any farther, you should know I've been to prison."

"What for?" Emily says.

"I stole a car. It was almost twenty years ago, and I haven't been in trouble since."

Emily is silent. She sits there chewing her knuckle.

"If that changes things, it changes things," Joe says. "I don't want to have any secrets."

"Secrets are good sometimes," Emily says.

"Not this time," Joe says.

Emily sighs. "See, man," she says, "why did you have to fucking say *that*?"

"What's wrong?"

"You're not the only one with a secret."

"Are *you* still married?"

"No, no, it's not that." A car passes by, radio blasting. When things quiet, Emily continues: "I wasn't working at a gallery in Chicago. I mean, I was, for a while, but then I was in a hospital."

"A hospital?" Joe says.

"A mental health facility."

"Why?"

"I moved to Chicago after Phoebe's dad took her to Austin, thinking I'd get a fresh start, but instead of doing the things I should have been doing to get her back, I drank too much and smoked too much weed and did coke all the time. I understand now I was severely depressed, but back then it seemed like things were never going to get any better, so I decided to kill myself. I took a bunch of pills and drank a bottle of vodka, but a friend found me and called 911."

She pauses and shakes her head. "This is so fucking embarrassing," she says. Joe takes her hand. "My parents put me in a hospital, and I spent three months there, getting my shit together. When I got out, my sister offered to let me stay with her."

"Did the hospital help? Do you feel better?" Joe asks her.

"Sure," she says.

"*Sure*'s not an answer."

She smiles sadly and traces the letters tattooed on his fingers. "How about, 'A little better every day'?" she says. "Is that enough?"

"Look at me," Joe says. She lifts her gaze to meet his. "None of what you told me changes how I feel about you."

"Yeah, right," she says.

"I mean it," Joe says.

She stares at him as if trying to read the truth in his eyes, then throws her arms around him and whispers, "Let's go." They sneak back to the guesthouse, where they fall onto the bed and pick up where they left off earlier. When the moment's right, Joe strips off her panties and slides her to the edge of the mattress, intending to go down on her, but she pulls him back on top and whispers, "Just put it in. I'm ready."

They're supposed to keep quiet so nobody in the main house catches on. When Emily comes, she clamps a hand over her mouth to stifle her moan. She goes into the bathroom afterward, and Joe steps outside for a smoke.

The main house is dark, and it's so silent and so still, Joe can hear the tobacco in his cigarette crackle as it burns. He marvels at how many more stars there are in the sky up here in the hills than down in the flats where he lives and thinks about how things have changed over the past couple days, what he's gotten himself into with Emily and the heroin and the gun. It makes him nervous. He's got to be careful not to let too much crazy into his life.

Emily's asleep when he goes back inside. He lies beside her on the bed and curves his body around hers.

He comes to later with Emily standing over him, wide-eyed and frantic. "You have to go," she says.

"What's wrong?" he asks her. The clock by the bed shows 3:30 a.m.

"I can't let my sister find you here."

"Okay. Relax."

"Please. You have to hurry."

He dresses quickly and checks his pockets for his phone, his wallet, his keys. Emily shoves him out the door, leaving him to creep down the side of the house by himself.

He drives home on deserted early-morning streets. At Vermont and Melrose he stops for a red light behind a white BMW. The BMW doesn't move when the light changes, so he taps his horn. The car continues to sit there. He goes around it, slowing to look at the driver. An Asian woman's lying with her cheek on the steering wheel. Her eyes are closed, and her mouth is open. She's wearing red lipstick.

Joe lowers the truck's passenger-side window and yells, "Hey!"

The woman doesn't stir.

Headlights appear in the truck's rearview mirror. There's a good chance it's a cop at this hour. Joe raises the window and drives off, feeling like it's the narrowest of getaways.

July 25, 11:33 p.m.

Who was it that didn't get laid enough beforehand in *your* marriage?

What do you mean?

It lasted less than a year. Who didn't get laid enough before, you or her?

That's a different story. Our problem was low self-esteem. We fucked a couple times in high school but didn't really get along, and four years later or whatever, when we hooked up again, both our lives sucked. I'd just been kicked out of the Marines and was dealing with that and having to move back to Burbank and living with my mom and sleeping in the bed I slept in as a kid with all my kid crap on the walls and all my kid clothes in the closet. Heather was miserable too. She was still living at home and still working at the same restaurant she worked at in high school. We started going out again, but it was no better the second time. We did okay when we were partying, but when we weren't, we didn't have anything to say to each other, and I felt more alone when I was with her than when I was by myself.

So why'd you get married?

I think it's because we both felt like no one else wanted us and that somehow made us perfect for each other. You want to be happy so bad, you fool yourself. You tell yourself things'll get better, but they don't. We got an apartment and set about torturing each other, shit like her slashing my tires and me lying about being

91

allergic to her cat and making her get rid of it. We were poison for each other and got sicker and sicker the longer we were together.

But the sex was awesome, right?

Yeah, right. She disgusted me, and I disgusted her. I never quit tapping all the ass I could get on the side, and she had an affair with a cook from her job and ended up pregnant. And that's how it ended: She moved in with him, and I went back to my mom's.

10: *SUNT LACRIMAE RERUM*

J ESUS STRETCHED HIS ARMS OUT WIDE," A TV PREACHER SHOUTS from behind Janey's door as Joe walks to the bathroom. "He let them drive spikes into his hands and feet. He let them thrust a spear into his side."

The swelling in Joe's foot has gone down. He leaves the bandage off after he showers so the wound can get air. Back in his room, he checks his phone. No message from Keith. Dude must be in deep shit. Also no messages from Breezy or Dave or any of the other people he's been hitting up for work. He'll be behind the bar at the Shorty again tonight but still texts Matt in hopes of clocking a few rides in the Prius before his shift begins. The guy's already out driving, though, so, all of a sudden there's a whole day to kill. It's after noon, but he texts Emily, *Good morning*. She doesn't reply.

He eats a bowl of Frosted Flakes, smokes half a joint he finds in an ashtray in the living room, and stretches out on the couch in front of the TV. He jumps from channel to channel in search of something that doesn't rub him the wrong way, finally settling on a cooking show. A soft-voiced woman is baking a pie. Stoned as hell, he decides he's going to bake Emily a pie. He's never baked one before, but he's sure there are videos on how to do it. A few minutes later the idea seems ridiculous. A few more minutes later he's forgotten the whole thing.

He's watching *The Shawshank Redemption* when Junior, Robert, and Candy troop in. They've been to Morongo Casino, and Candy won a hundred dollars.

"Take us to Target," she says to Junior. "I'll buy you whatever you want."

Her jubilation grates on Joe. He retreats to his room for a pre-work nap. The front door slams, and things quiet down again. *She must have convinced him,* Joe thinks as he's dozing off. *She couldn't have convinced me.*

He wakes smelling smoke and opens his eyes to see flickering orange flames outside the little window instead of pink stucco. It's all adrenaline after that. He retrieves his bank from under the mattress. His wallet and keys are in his jeans. Pulling on a shirt and shoes, he grabs his phone, dashes into the hall, and pounds on doors.

"Fire!" he yells. "Fire!"

Janey opens her door a crack and peeks out at him.

"The house is on fire!" he says.

"What's that smell?" she says.

"It's fucking smoke," he shouts, gesturing at the acrid haze filling the air. "Get out now."

She goes from frightened to hysterical in an instant, throwing open her door and running for the stairs with a wordless wail. Joe takes the steps to the attic two at a time. The smoke's thicker up here, stings his eyes. Leland's door opens before he can knock, and the dude pushes past him, notebooks clutched to his chest. Joe follows him down and notices that Paulo's door is still shut. He bangs on it again and tries the knob. It's locked. Drawing back a leg, he kicks hard next to the deadbolt. Rotten wood splinters, and the door flies open. A Brazilian flag on the wall, dumbbells on the floor next to the bed, but no Paulo.

He flies down the stairs to the living room, where he's walloped by a blast of heat. The kitchen's fully engulfed, and flames reach greedily for him. He dodges and knocks on Junior's door, on Robert and Candy's, not waiting to see if anyone answers.

He's coughing when he runs out the front door but heads straight for the backyard without slowing down. The whole rear of the house is on fire. Black smoke billows up to blot out the sun, and the shadow it casts ripples across the dead grass like dark water. Joe ducks into the shed. He takes the heroin from the box of decorations and shoves it down his pants and slides the Glock in his waistband. The gun and dope are all he has that's worth anything, and he doesn't want to lose them.

He tries not to look sketchy on his way to the F-150, walking past the fire trucks screaming up the street. His hands are shaking so badly, it takes him multiple tries to dial in the combinations for the locks on the toolbox. He hides the pistol and dope there and grabs a bottle of water. His throat hurts when he drinks it down.

When he returns to the house, the firefighters have their hoses hooked up and are spraying water on the flames. A small crowd has formed across the street, everyone filming the blaze with their phones. Joe joins Janey and Leland there. Janey goggles at the fire while praying silently, hands clasped at her waist, lips moving a mile a minute. Leland's face is blank. He could be staring at a wall. Everyone else is sneaking looks at the three of them, getting a thrill out of watching them watch their lives go up in smoke.

Junior's Jeep screeches to a stop at a row of orange plastic cones blocking the street. He, Robert, and Candy spill out. A cop warns them to stay back.

"That's my fucking house," Junior says.

"Let the fire department do its job," the cop says.

Junior shuffles back and forth on his side of the cones, chanting, "Fuck, fuck, fuck," under his breath.

Robert and Candy come over to stand next to Joe. Robert lifts his phone above the crowd and pans from the fire trucks to the house. "What happened?" he says.

Joe tells him how he woke to flames. "We barely got out," he says.

"I dreamed this," Candy says. "It was rats that started it."

More fire trucks arrive, and a news chopper circles overhead. Robert tracks it with his camera. "What station is that?" he says. "Can you tell?"

The deluge from the hoses finally drowns the fire, and the smoke goes from black clouds to white wisps that get hung up in the fronds of the palm trees lining the street. Joe's shunted from firefighter to firefighter as he tries to find out when he'll be able to go inside the house to retrieve his belongings. The final word comes from a tall Black man sweating under a yellow helmet: tomorrow at the earliest.

It's time for Joe to go to work. He checks in with Junior and the others. Nobody's figured out where they're going or what they're going to do. Joe leaves them sitting on the curb, staring numbly at their phones.

Emily texts as he's parking Keith's truck in the little lot behind the bar.

Sorry I freaked last night.

The house I live in is on fire right now, he texts back.

His phone rings a second later.

"What are you talking about?" Emily says.

He tells her the story.

"Oh my god," she says when he finishes. "What happens now?"

"I'm gonna work my shift," he says.

"Where will you sleep?"

"I'll find somewhere."

"Come here," Emily says. "Fuck my sister. This is an emergency."

"It's cool," Joe says, not wanting to get into the middle of that. "I've got plenty of options."

Even after he washes up in the men's room and changes into one of the bar's swag T-shirts, he still smells like smoke. It's a slow night, quiet, but there's tension in the air that keeps him on edge. He attributes it to the scare the fire gave him, and stays busy organizing the storeroom and restocking behind the bar, trying not to think too much.

Mitchell hangs out longer and gets drunker than he usually does. He sings along loudly to the jukebox until Joe tells him to shut up. He spills a beer attempting a magic trick. "You're a fucking know-nothing turd," he yells at some guy from New York, arguing about baseball.

"Fuck you, Boston" is the guy's response.

Joe steps in and says to cool it or he'll cut them both off. The guy from New York goes into the back room to play pool with a buddy.

"What's up with you tonight?" Joe asks Mitchell.

"My dad died this morning," Mitchell replies.

"That sucks," Joe says. "I'm sorry to hear it."

"He shot himself."

Joe reaches for the Bushmills and pours the man a double.

"You too," Mitchell says. "Drink with me."

Joe's been holding off, wanting to keep a clear head with so much going on, but it'd be an insult to deny a request like this.

Mitchell's toast when they tap glasses is *"Sunt lacrimae rerum."*

"What's that?" Joe asks him.

"There are tears at the heart of things."

Baba, at the other end of the bar, motions Joe over. Trying to be discreet, he points at the floor without looking down. A mouse is stuck in the glue trap next to the ice machine, stuck tight, lying on its side but still struggling now and then. Joe drops a towel over the trap so the customers won't see and picks it up and carries it out to the patio, a dead-end, gated alley behind the building. A guy and a girl are smoking and laughing at something stupid someone named Lilly did. They ignore Joe as he walks down to the gate, sets the trap on the ground, and lights his own cigarette.

The mouse shudders under the towel, rattling the trap. Joe takes his time finishing his smoke, stubs it out, then picks up the cinderblock used to prop the gate open during deliveries. Standing over the trap, he slams the block down onto it. When he lifts the block and nudges the towel with his foot, there's no reaction from the mouse. He picks up the trap, towel and all, and tosses it into the dumpster.

Shouts from inside bring him running back. Mitchell and the guy he was arguing with are wrestling on the floor. The guy has Mitchell in a choke hold, and Mitchell's gasping and gurgling and trying to twist loose. Both fools are smeared with blood. Teddy, the big Black bouncer, takes hold of the guy from New York, and Joe grabs Mitchell. They separate after a few tugs.

Baba reports that the guy snuck up on Mitchell and sucker-punched him. Mitchell lunges at the guy, yelling, "I'll fucking kill him," but Joe easily holds him back. The blood's coming from Mitchell's nose. He sucks some into his mouth and spits it at the guy. Joe spins him so he's facing the other way and tells him to knock it off.

"You're eighty-sixed," Teddy informs the guy from New York as he manhandles him to the front door. "Don't come back." The guy's buddy gets salty, so he's booted too.

Joe pushes Mitchell toward the bathroom and stands by while he washes the blood off his face. The bright red drops on the white porcelain of the sink look like phony horror movie gore. Mitchell starts to cry.

"My dad was a drunk like me," he says.

Joe hands him his scally, which he retrieved from the floor. Mitchell pulls himself together, plugs his nose with toilet paper, and walks back out to the bar, where Manuel is mopping up the blood. Mitchell orders another drink, but Joe tells him it's time to go.

The night crawls by so slowly after this, Joe feels like he's stoned even though he isn't. Every song that comes on the jukebox hits him hard. "There's already someone sleeping on the couch at my place, but you can crash on the floor," Baba says, his lack of enthusiasm obvious. Joe lets him off the hook by saying he already has somewhere to go.

He drives to Junior's when he gets off. The house is a dark, forbidding bulk against the night sky. Yellow caution tape is threaded in the low chain-link fence that separates the yard from the sidewalk. UNSAFE. DO NOT ENTER OR OCCUPY warns a red sign on the gate. Joe makes sure nobody's watching before opening the gate and slipping through it.

He creeps around to the backyard. The ground's muddy, and the air smells like smoke. The rear wall of the house has been scorched from foundation to roof, and most of the siding has been torn away, exposing the charred bones of the framing. Singed wood and soggy insulation are piled everywhere.

The back entrance has been boarded up with a sheet of plywood. Joe gets a stepladder and a screwdriver from the shed. He places the ladder under the kitchen window, which he knows doesn't lock. Wedging the screwdriver into the space between the sash and the sill, he's able to raise the sash enough to get his fingers under it and lift it the rest of the way.

The light from his phone shows the kitchen burned to the studs. Clumps of sodden plaster from the collapsed ceiling litter what's left of the floor, most of which has dropped into the basement, leaving only the joists intact.

Joe slithers through the window and carefully lowers himself from the counter to stand with his left foot on one joist, his right on another. They support his weight, so he shuffles along, avoiding looking down into the bottomless basement that yawns beneath him. Reaching a section of unburned floor, he dashes across it to the hallway.

The front half of the house is in better shape, mainly water damage. The living room looks like it did when he was relaxing there earlier except the furniture is soaked and the TV is lying screen-down on the floor. The stairs to his room are covered with debris, and where the ceiling used to be, a patch of purple sky is visible through a hole in the roof. He climbs to the second floor one cautious step at a time, placing his feet in the firefighters' boot prints.

The door to Janey's room is open, to Paulo's, to his. Janey's room's the only one that burned. That might be what's left of her bed there, and maybe the other heap was her dresser. The windows have been busted out, and water drips from exposed rafters.

His room, toward the front of the house, didn't even get wet. He crams his clothes, sleeping bag, and kit bag into his backpack. The rest of his stuff—flip-flops, a manila envelope containing his discharge and parole documents, a flashlight, a book on poker strategy he's never read—he tosses into a garbage bag.

The house is a teardown for sure. He bids farewell to it on his way down the stairs. *Adiós, you fucking dump. Good riddance, you rat trap.* He leaves through the front door, which is locked but not boarded up.

Returning to the F-150, he spreads his sleeping bag on the back seat and settles on top of it. He's too keyed up to sleep, though. And the noise! Maybe it's the way the breeze is blowing, but the Hollywood Freeway half a mile away is so loud, it's as if he's parked on the shoulder. And then there are the sirens, the train horns, the choppers. About four o'clock he thinks he hears someone breaking into the toolbox. He sits up, shouts, "Hey!" and gets out to check. Nobody's there. He takes the pistol from the box and brings it into the cab, but even with the gun in easy reach, he still jumps at every little sound.

July 31, 1:02 a.m.

Tell me about your time in prison.

What time in prison?

You've mentioned prison a few times. Were you bullshitting?

No, I wasn't bullshitting.

You don't want to talk about it?

I did ten months in Chino.

For what?

For standing up for myself. Ah, fuck, here's the story. After I split with Heather I went on the kind of bender you go on when shit like that happens, the kind where you stay as fucked up as possible for as long as possible so you don't have to deal with what went wrong and why. I took a bong rip as soon as I woke up every morning, cracked a beer, and the day proceeded from there. Now what you find out when you're living like that is that lots of other people are too. Walk into any dive bar at noon, and you'll have a drinking buddy. A lot of the people you meet are running out their unemployment like I was or on the government's tit because they're crazy or crippled, but not all of them are fuckups. I hung out with lawyers, doctors, actors, an architect, an engineer—all kinds of drunks and dopers. Some were useless, some were evil, some were so close to dying, you could see their ghosts sitting next to them, and some were as good as people get. Tod, the guy whose garage I was sleeping in at the end of that particular toot, was one of the evil ones. He only let me crash at his place to have someone to fuck with. He'd pay for booze—he had money coming from somewhere—for coke, for food, but in exchange I had to take his shit. He called me retard, Joe Dirt, Freddy the Freeloader. He'd tell people I was his slave and make me fetch beers for them and light their smokes. "Let my slave do that." I ended up beating the fuck out of him. I broke his nose and knocked out a couple of his teeth and took his car and headed for San Diego, thinking I'd sell it in TJ. Not a smart move, considering I was so fucked up I had to close one eye to see straight enough to drive. The CHP lit me up before I hit Downey, but I made them chase me until I ran out of gas. I tried booking it on foot, but they caught me pretty quick.

Was it on TV?

Fuck yeah. For fifty miles I was a superstar. I ended up pleading to felony GTA, got sixteen months, and did ten. Is there any more whiskey?

We finished it.

If I go in the kitchen and find more, I'm gonna give you some of what I gave Tod.

You didn't learn your lesson?

What is this, fucking Sunday school?

11: TERRORISTS

Exhaustion finally drags Joe under, but he doesn't sleep long. A fly trapped in the truck, buzzing and bouncing off the windshield, wakes him, and the rising sun quickly turns the cab into a sweatbox. He stumbles out onto the street and pisses in an empty lot, his back giving him all kinds of hell. In the old days, he could sleep anywhere and pop right up in the morning, ready to rock. Not anymore.

A red fire department SUV is parked in front of the house when he drives down the hill. Junior, Robert, and Candy are standing there with Starbucks cups in their hands, talking to a firefighter. Joe gets out and walks over in time to catch Junior yelling, "Bullshit, man! That's bullshit!"

"I didn't write the law," the firefighter says. "An inspector has to certify it's safe before you can go in."

"When's that gonna happen?"

"Hopefully later today. There's a backlog."

"And what are we supposed to do until then? All our stuff's in there."

"You might want to make arrangements to stay somewhere else."

"Do you know what caused the fire?" Candy asks. "Was it a rat?"

The firefighter ignores the question to go back and forth with Junior about the inspection. When he realizes nothing he says is going to mollify him, he retreats to his rig and sits staring at his phone.

"We'll wait him out," Junior says. "He can't hang around all day."

"Fuck it," Robert says. "Let's bum-rush the place."

Joe doesn't mention sneaking in last night, doesn't want to stir the pot.

"Whose truck is that?" Junior asks about the F-150.

"A buddy's," Joe says.

"What are *you* gonna do?" Robert asks him.

"I've got a job today," he says. "I'm on my way to work."

This is a lie. He's not at all sure what he's going to do, but whatever it is won't involve these clowns. Now isn't the time to ask Junior for a refund of his rent, so he wishes everyone good luck and splits.

He buys coffee at McDonald's and drinks it sitting on a bench by the lake in Echo Park. The homeless who camp there under the palm trees are starting their day. They crawl out of their tents and stagger past wary, muttering geese to the public restrooms, where a security guard monitors the growing line. First cigarettes are lit, first beers opened, first fixes cooked up. A haze of dope smoke gives the palms the ghostly quality they have in old photos of the place.

A lunatic smeared with filth and wearing only a greasy

loincloth stands next to the path that circles the lake. He scares the hell out of the runners and dog walkers by bellowing, "I hate you!" at the top of his lungs as they pass by. The yelling gets to Joe. He tells the guy to knock it off.

"Fuck you!" the lunatic replies, then plops down on the grass to groom himself like a chimp, sniffing whatever he picks out of his beard before flicking it away.

Joe's phone rings.

"Where'd you end up sleeping?" Emily asks.

"A guy I work with let me crash at his place," Joe says.

"Is that where you'll be staying now?"

"I'm figuring things out."

"Let me buy you breakfast," Emily says.

Joe meets her at a hipped-up diner in Los Feliz. He washed at the park's outdoor sink and changed his shirt but still worries she can smell the last twenty-four hours on him when they hug. They sit across from each other in a booth, and she makes him tell her again about the fire. He finishes up as their food arrives.

"Do you have everything you need?" she says. "We can go shopping."

"I'm good," he says.

"What about money?" she says. "Do you have enough?"

The question pisses Joe off. "Don't ask me that," he snaps.

"Why not?" Emily says.

"Because my problems aren't yours."

"And mine aren't yours, but all I've done since we met is lay them on you."

"That's different," Joe says, digging into his pancakes.

"Okay, fine, but it's supposed to work both ways," Emily says.

"Can we talk about something else?" Joe says.

Emily reaches across the table and wraps one of her index fingers around one of his. She asks if he'll be looking for a new place in the same neighborhood. He tells her he's thinking about moving to the Valley, where rent'll be cheaper. He might even be able to swing his own apartment there.

A rambunctious toddler dashes across the restaurant. She ends up on Emily's side of the booth, staring up at her.

"Hello there," Emily says.

The child's mother hurries over, apologetic.

"She's fine," Emily assures her, and addresses the baby again. "Where were you running to? Or were you just running?"

Joe gets a text from Wahid: Is he free to work at the store from noon to eight or nine? He's off at the bar tonight, so texts back, *Absolutely dude.*

Emily picks up the baby and sits her in her lap.

"What a doll you are with those big blue eyes."

Out of nowhere, the kid starts to cry.

"I better take her," the mother says.

Emily passes the baby to her, saying, "Something must have scared her."

"Shhhhh," the mother whispers in the little girl's ear, but she won't be calmed. The mother turns to her skater-daddy husband, jerks her head toward the door, and carries the child outside.

"She thinks it was my fault," Emily says.

"What are you talking about?" Joe says.

"She thinks something I did made her baby cry."

"Kids cry all the time," Joe says.

"I have a kid," Emily says. "I know how to hold one."

She's working herself up. Joe tries to distract her by telling her about Wahid and his family, how the first job the dad got in the States was at a dildo factory in Chatsworth. It takes him a while to shift her focus, but he eventually gets her talking about a documentary she made about a Chinese restaurant.

She insists on paying for the meal, then they walk up the street and go into a bookstore. She browses, and he pretends to, picking up random books and leafing through them.

"Do you read?" she asks him.

What's he going to say in a bookstore, everyone there hearing the question and listening for his answer? "When I have time" is what he comes up with.

When he leaves her at her car afterward, she says, "I know you're a tough guy, but please tell me if I can help you out somehow."

"I will," he says.

"No, you won't," she says.

The liquor store doesn't have a parking lot, and the closest spot Joe can find is in front of a tenement two blocks away. It's not even noon, but dope dealers are already working the stoop. Their lookout whistles when Joe gets out of the truck. There's no way he's leaving behind his backpack and the trash bag containing the rest of his stuff. He also takes the gun and heroin out of the toolbox and buries them in the pack.

Wahid's going to a funeral. His uncle was hit by a car in Koreatown.

"Some drunk bitch in a BMW," Wahid says. "She drove all the way back to USC with his blood on her windshield and was in jail only two hours."

Joe stashes his bags in the back room. The shift kicks off slow, four or five customers an hour. Beer, cigarettes, lottery tickets. Joe plays poker on his phone, watches *Judge Judy* on the TV tucked under the counter, and pages through a Ferrari magazine he finds in a drawer, Wahid dreaming big.

Things pick up when school lets out and kids come in to buy candy, chips, and sodas. Whenever there are more than two kids in the store at once, Joe steps out from behind the counter and pretends to straighten merchandise in order to make sure they don't fill their backpacks with Takis and Skittles. A tough little *chica* with green hair calls him out for this, asks what he's looking at.

"I'm restocking," he says.

"Bullshit," the girl says. "You're profiling us. The terrorists that own this place are always up our asses."

"How do you know they're terrorists?" Joe says.

One of the two boys with the girl ululates loudly. The other says, "They're Muslims. They hate us. Don't you know anything?"

"Yeah, I do," Joe says. "I fought in Iraq."

"So fucking what?" the girl says, to raucous laughter from her pals. She sets her Mountain Dew and Doritos on the counter. "Get your ass over here and ring me up."

Joe lets it go. He was a shithead, too, at their age.

After the schoolkids come men stopping in after work for Tecate tallboys and the cans of beans and quarts of milk their wives have texted them to pick up. Powdered with drywall dust, spattered with paint, sweat-stained, and dog-tired, they still manage a laugh for a friend's stupid joke and a respectful *"Buenas tardes"* for the old church ladies dressed in black.

During a lull, Joe calls Keith. He was going to wait until the dude contacted him, but in light of his sudden homelessness, he wants to know how long he's going to have the truck. The call goes to voice mail, so he texts *What's cracking?* No response.

At six he zaps a frozen burrito in the store's microwave and eats it at the register. He gets sleepy after that, nearly dozing off while staring at the security cam monitor, so he downs a Red Bull and a Five-Hour Energy Shot. The caffeine does a number on him. His mouth's so dry, every swallow is an effort, and his hands shake as he counts out change.

Wahid gets back at eight thirty and pays him off. He tries to use one of the twenties to buy a twelve-pack of beer, but Wahid says, "No, my friend, take it, take it."

It's just about full dark. The streetlights have come on. Joe's relieved to find the truck where he parked it. Lots of people besides the dealers are out now, the whole neighborhood. A ragtag pickup soccer game swirls in the middle of the street, old men, young men, kids all getting in on the action. Laughter and joyous shouts ring out when a mother leaves her stroller to stand in as a goalie. She goes head to head with a fat loudmouth and blocks every kick he tries to get past her.

Joe stows the garbage bag and his backpack in the cab, then opens a beer and leans against the truck to watch the game. A *paletero* hawks popsicles from his cart. An old woman slices a mango and feeds it to a chihuahua wearing a frilly red dress. Twenty different songs blare from twenty different radios.

A scream rises above the din. The years Joe's spent in bars tell him it's trouble. A girl and two boys spill out onto the stoop of the building he's parked in front of. The boys are fighting. One's getting the best of the other, punching him repeatedly in the face, but Joe glimpses a knife in the other kid's hand.

The girl screams again, and people yell for the kid to drop the weapon. The guy he's fighting, though, goads him, spreading his arms wide, slapping himself on the chest, and shouting, "*Mátame, culero, mátame.*" The kid with the knife lunges.

Joe drops his beer and moves toward the stoop, yelling NO! along with everyone else. Two more kids charge out of the building and tackle the guy with the knife. The knife flies out of his hand and lands at Joe's feet.

The crowd whistles and cheers as a siren approaches. Joe panics, remembering the gun and drugs in his backpack. He runs around to the driver's side of the truck, presses the fob to unlock the door, and climbs inside. His head's buzzing as he pulls away from the curb. A couple of the soccer players jump out of his way, one of them yelping and slapping the fender as the truck passes by.

July 19, 12:50 a.m.

What are you watching?

A video of a pit bull that's scared of a cat.

Hoot Gibson in *Who Shit on my Saddle?*

What?

That's something my grandpa used to say. I'd be watching
TV, and he'd go, "What's that show? Hoot Gibson in
Who Shit on My Saddle?" He was a big old cowboy from
Texas, a Nam vet named Buck, who chewed tobacco
and carried an empty Coke can to spit in. "I'm so hungry, I could eat the asshole out of a dead skunk" was
another of his sayings, and I remember being like eight
or nine and him telling me stories about screwing
hookers in the navy. "You still got your cherry?" he
asked one. "No, I don't," she said. "That's okay," he
told her. "You still got the box it came in." I didn't even
know what that meant. My mom and him didn't get
along. She blamed him and my grandma for pushing
her to marry my dad. Her and my grandma didn't talk,
but Buck would bring over a little money or some groceries every once in a while. He was the only person in
my family I could stand. He only made it to fifty-five
though. Lung cancer. I'm hoping to beat that.

12: COMFORT INN

Joe drives aimlessly until he calms down. West on Wilshire to La Brea, La Brea to Hollywood, south on Vine, east on Santa Monica until it curves up to Sunset in Silver Lake. He decides he needs to get off the street, get a good night's sleep, and ends up at a Comfort Inn on the edge of Echo Park, a stucco box with a Thai restaurant on the ground floor and two floors of rooms above. He chooses it because of its underground parking garage, a place where the truck will be safe. Handing over a hundred bucks to the desk clerk hurts. He's too worn out to go looking for somewhere cheaper though.

The room's nothing special, but it's a hell of a lot more luxe than his cell at Junior's. He wipes the gun and stashes it and the heroin under the bed. If anybody for some reason searching the room were to ask, "What do we have here?" well, hey, that shit must belong to whoever stayed here last night.

Feeling clever, he turns on the TV, cranks up the air conditioner, and opens a beer.

He's outside having a smoke on a bus bench when he calls Emily. He doesn't tell her about getting shaken up by the knife fight, just says he was beat after working all day and splurged on a room.

"Can I come over?" she says.

He was planning on going to sleep, but the thought of seeing her gives him a second wind.

"Do you *want* to come over?" he says.

"I'll be there in half an hour."

She texts *I'm here* when she arrives, and Joe walks down to the lobby to bring her up. She's carrying a bottle of wine and looks cute in her cowboy boots and sundress. They're all over each other as soon as the door closes behind them, his hands on her tits, hers on his cock. He worries he'll pop as soon as he sticks it in but manages to hold off by changing positions and slowing down when he gets close. Finally though—her on her back, legs raised, moaning—he cums so hard he blacks out for a second and will swear forever after it was one of the best fucks of his life.

Emily opens the wine and drinks it out of one of the room's plastic cups. He sticks to beer. They watch Jimmy Fallon interview a singer, a girl neither of them has heard of. Emily finds one of the girl's videos on YouTube and tries to show it to Joe, but he closes his eyes and turns away, playing at stubbornness. Emily sticks the phone in his face.

"Come on," she says. "She's hot."

"She's bullshit," he says.

He wishes things could stay like this, the two of them, sated and silly, lying in bed with enough of a buzz that regular life seems a long way off.

★　★　★

He wakes at three a.m. with no memory of having fallen asleep. Emily's standing at the window, looking out. A string of firetrucks is passing by on Sunset below, sirens yowling, horns blaring. Their lights swirl over Emily's naked body.

"Don't tell me this place is burning down too," he says.

Emily picks up the wine bottle from the nightstand. She tips it into her glass, but it's empty.

"Can't sleep?" Joe asks her.

"I stopped taking Lexapro," she says. "My system's still adjusting."

"That shit's tricky."

"Were you ever on it?"

"I've been on everything once or twice."

Crawling across the bed, Emily says, "Thank God there's something else that calms me down."

They fuck slowly this time, working up to it and drawing it out when they get there. It's light outside when Joe wakes again. Emily's sitting cross-legged beside him. She runs her fingers over the tattoos on his chest.

"What's this one?" she asks.

He lifts his head off the pillow to see where she's pointing.

"A map of Iraq," he says. "Marine Corps shit. And that's a crappy M-16 above it."

"And this one?"

"The solar system. A guy once asked me to name all the planets, and I felt stupid when I couldn't. That'll never happen again."

"And here?"

"That's the devil sitting on a toilet."

"Because?"

Joe sits up. "Freak show's over," he says.

Emily's dressed and texting furiously when he comes out of the bathroom after taking a shower.

"It's my sister," she says. "Give me a second to finish telling her to fuck off."

The hotel serves a free breakfast—bagels, yogurt, instant oatmeal—but Emily says, "We can do better than that." They walk a couple blocks on Sunset to a Cuban coffee shop. The nine a.m. AA meeting in the community space next door has just ended, so they have to wait in line behind all the alkies ordering triple cafecitos and guava-cream cheese pastries. Joe goes for bacon, eggs, and cheese on a croissant. "Just eggs and cheese for me," Emily says. They take the food out to one of the tables on the sidewalk.

"I lived around the corner there back before rents went crazy," Joe says. "I knew a dude who spent three years of his life sitting right here. Every time I passed by, any time of day, he was at this table. He knew every bum, every AAer, every rock star, and every porn actress in the neighborhood. He had to say hi and bullshit with so many people, you could never have a decent conversation with him."

"Where is he now?" Emily says.

"His band broke up and he moved back to Detroit."

"I can relate," Emily says. "I've left so many places because things fell apart."

"See, I'm the opposite," Joe says. "Shit's fallen apart for me a hundred times here, and I've never once thought about leaving."

"Why not?"

"Where am I gonna go?"

"You've never lived anywhere else?"

"Iraq, prison."

"Come to Nicaragua with me," Emily says. "We'll both learn to surf."

"Sure," Joe says. "We'll leave after I get off from the bar tonight."

"I'll go to my sister's and get my clothes and meet you there."

"I bet you would."

A little dog wanders over from the next table to beg for a handout. Emily bends to pet it. "I love your puppy," she says to the guy at the other end of the animal's leash.

"You can have him," the guy jokes.

"It's tempting," Emily says. "But we're moving to Nicaragua."

On their way back to the motel they pass a weed store on the second floor of a grungy mini-mall.

"I need something to knock me out at night," Emily says.

They watch a Bugs Bunny cartoon on a TV in the waiting room until they're buzzed into the store. The guy who helps them has a shaved head and the word FURIOUS tattooed over his left eye. Emily takes her time, sniffing and scrutinizing a variety of buds before opting for an eighth of something called Cherry Girl.

"Indica twenty-seven point one percent," Joe reads off the jar's label. "That'll do ya."

Outside, it's cooler than it's been in a week. A breeze is blowing off the ocean, pushing all the smog out to Riverside. Joe's thinking he and Emily might take a hike in Griffith Park, but she says she's got to go have it out with her sister in person.

Checkout's fast approaching when he gets back to the room. He reluctantly calls down and arranges to stay another night. He should be sleeping in the truck while he has it, saving his cash, but it's too risky with the gun and heroin. The smart thing would be to toss both, but that'd be like throwing away money. He has a better idea. He texts Danny Bones *Got something you might be interested in*, figuring even if the dude doesn't mess with junk, he'll know someone who does. As for the Glock, that'll be easy to get rid of. Everybody's always looking for guns.

He sends more texts and makes a few calls telling people about the fire and asking if they have a line on somewhere for him to stay, temporary or permanent. It's mostly "I got nothing, but I'll ask around," although Stu offers to let him pitch a tent in his yard, and a guy he's done some painting for says his brother rents part of his house in El Monte, but he'd have to share a room with three other people. Joe hopes it doesn't come to that.

It's Baba's night off, so Shannon's behind the bar. Her husband and some friends come in around nine, and she leaves most of the work to Joe while she hangs with them. Her husband's an actor who was on a sitcom for two seasons ten years ago, and he's been running on the fumes of that ever since. Shannon still acts like a groupie when she's around the stuck-up little punk, gets all starry-eyed and pretends she hasn't heard every one of his stupid stories a thousand times. Joe's pissed at having to pick up the slack while she socializes, but he can't call her on it when she's about to bring him back full-time.

Fortunately, it's slow for a Friday. At ten thirty the DJ is spinning to a nearly empty dance floor. Joe's able to keep up with the orders and also goof off with Claudia, the server working the tables. She's twenty-four, with Bettie Page bangs and a ring in her nose. They play a game they invented called Laugh Factory, where they take turns telling each other bad jokes.

Joe's up.

"What do you call a pig that knows karate?" he asks while she's clearing a tray of empty bottles and glasses.

"Uh, what?" she says.

"A pork chop."

"Oof. I need two Captain and Cokes, and have you ever heard of a King Alphonse?"

"Can't do it. I don't have cream."

"Three Captain and Cokes then."

Danny's reply comes at midnight: *I'll be at Taco Taco tomorrow night.*

I don't get off until 2, Joe texts back.

If I'm there, I'm there, Danny replies.

Shannon's husband splits around one, and she's suddenly all business, wiping down the bar like Joe's been neglecting it and repositioning the pint glasses he just stacked. She shoves him aside when Claudia comes up with an order and sets about making the drinks at superspeed. Probably did a bump.

"What does a vegan zombie eat?" Claudia asks Joe.

"No idea," Joe says.

"Grrraaaaiiiinnnsss!"

He gets back to the motel at two thirty and is dead asleep at three fifteen when his phone rings.

"I'm downstairs," Emily says. "Can I come up?"

He pulls on his jeans and goes down to meet her. She couldn't sleep so took a drive and wound up here. "I'm not stalking you, I swear," she says. They smoke a joint, watch some TV, and fuck to a *Petticoat Junction* laugh track. The sun's blazing through a rip in the blackout curtain before Joe gets to sleep again.

July 20, 11:24 p.m.

Come on, dude, cover your mouth when you yawn.

I was out late with my boys last night.

Your boys? You've got boys? Did you guys have a circle jerk? Did you have to eat the cracker?

You've got boys, too.

I don't hang out with guys. I'm into women.

You don't have any guy friends?

Do you know your chances of getting laid if you show up at a bar with a bunch of your buddies? Take it from a bartender, slim and none. If you want to get laid, fly solo.

It's not always about getting laid. Sometimes I just want to go somewhere and have drinks with friends and watch a game.

Not me.

You only go out to pick up women?

I don't go out much at all anymore. If I'm not working, making money, I'm sleeping.

So is this work, what we're doing?

The goal is to get rich, right? When you turn my stories into gold? Do you think I'm here because I like your company?

13: IF YOU MEET THE BUDDHA, KILL THE BUDDHA

Joe gets up to piss at nine and sees a text from Grady Gonzalez, one of the people he's been bugging for job leads. Grady wants to know if he's available this morning to help him move some sand and gravel from his driveway into his backyard, four or five hours' work for a hundred dollars. The message came in half an hour ago, and Joe calls back to see if the offer's still good.

"I could get a guy from in front of Home Depot, but I thought I'd ask you first," Grady says.

"I'll be there by ten," Joe assures him.

He's been talking in the bathroom with the door shut so as not to wake Emily, but she's sitting up in bed when he comes out. He tells her to go back to sleep until checkout time.

"Where are you staying tonight?" she asks him.

"With a friend," he says. "It's dumb for me to waste money on motels."

"I'll pay for another night here," she says.

"Forget it," he says.

"I'm not doing it for you," she says. "I can't deal with my sister this morning, and I just want to sleep all day. Go do your work and come back and hang with me."

Joe gets dressed. When Emily goes into the bathroom, he takes the gun and dope from under the bed and puts them in his backpack in case she has to change rooms.

"You *are* coming back, aren't you?" she says when she sees the pack slung over his shoulder.

"As fast as I can," he says, and gives her a kiss before heading out. A girl is clearing away the free breakfast in the lobby, but he's able to snag a banana and a plastic-wrapped Danish, and the girl lets him fill a foam cup with coffee.

Grady lives in Highland Park in a neighborhood of shabby 1960s tract homes that are being renovated, one by one, by flippers. He's got a big biker beard and belly, slicked-back biker hair, and tattoos, but he's into cars, not motorcycles, and is always in the middle of restoring one or two junkers. He proudly shows off his latest project when Joe arrives, a 1963 Galaxie he bought for two grand and hopes to sell for 50K when he finishes cherrying it.

He offers Joe coffee, but Joe says he's good. Grady is friends with Keith, so Joe asks if he's seen him lately.

"Nah, man," Grady says. "Not since he moved out to Norco or wherever."

Joe leaves it at that, doesn't mention the overdose and arrest.

Grady's replacing some of the grass in his backyard with pea gravel and big, jagged rocks. A zen garden, he calls it. "You contemplate it, and it chills you out." Joe pretends to look at the photo of another such garden in Japan that Grady pulls up on his phone, but the truth is, the sun's too bright for him to see it, and all he really wants to do is start work so he can get back to Emily.

The area for the garden has been cleared down to dirt and covered with landscape fabric. There's a pile of sand on the driveway and a pile of gravel. They start with the sand. One of them fills a wheelbarrow and pushes it down the side of the house, the other spreads the dumped sand and tamps it. They switch jobs every ten loads.

Joe gives himself over to the rhythm of the work. He always feels better when he's sweating instead of thinking. Fifteen scoops to fill the wheelbarrow, thirty steps to the backyard, don't bash the rainspouts. It's another hot day, but drifting clouds occasionally obscure the sun, tempering its intensity.

During one of Joe's turns spreading and tamping, the sliding glass door to the kitchen opens and three dogs and a pack of kids run out, a sudden, screeching explosion of pent-up energy.

"What the hell are you doing?" a woman yells from inside the house. "Get back in here!"

A wheezy French bulldog trots over to Joe, sniffs his shoe, and squats to pee on the sand. A girl of about eight picks up the dog and says, "Bad Betty!"

"When you gotta go, you gotta go," Joe says.

"Is my dad paying you?" a boy in a Star Wars T-shirt asks him.

"Would you do this for free?" he replies.

"I wouldn't do it for a million dollars," the kid says.

Two other boys swing foam swords while another girl

dances on a patch of just-smoothed sand. The woman who yelled steps out onto the patio.

"I said get inside!" she shouts.

Grady rounds the corner of the house with another load of sand. He empties the wheelbarrow and says, "Listen to your mom. We're working here." He tries to herd the kids inside, but they scamper away from him. "What's your problem?" he yells at the woman, his wife. "Take them to your *tia*'s."

The wife flips him off. Working together, they get the kids behind glass again.

"Sorry about that," Grady says to Joe. "They're fucking crazy all the time."

"How many do you have?" Joe says.

"Six, man, can you believe it? I'll be working till the day I drop."

One of the dogs, standing on its hind legs, scratches at the slider and barks its head off.

When the layer of sand is tamped to level, Joe and Grady wheel back the gravel that goes on top of it, another two hours with beer and cigarette breaks. They then place the rocks according to a plan Grady has drawn.

"It's gonna have bonsai trees too," Grady says.

As a finishing touch, he carefully rakes an undulating pattern into the gravel that's supposed to resemble ripples in water.

Joe's stomach is growling by the time Grady pays him off. He thinks about driving through Taco Bell but goes directly to the Comfort Inn instead. Emily looks like she just woke up when she comes down to get him, her hair tousled, her eyelids heavy. Or maybe she's high.

"I got an extra key," she says, and hands him a card.

When they get to the room, she falls onto the bed and holds out her arms. "Come here," she says.

"I'm filthy," Joe replies.

She licks his cheek.

He asks if she's had lunch, and she says she's been asleep since he left. Neither of them wants to go out, so they order a pizza. Joe showers while they're waiting for it to arrive. They eat sprawled on the bed, watching an old *Law & Order*. Emily points out one of the actors and says he's her daughter's godfather.

"We knew him in Malibu," she says. "He hit on me once."

"Before or after he was the godfather?" Joe says.

"You don't believe me," Emily says.

"Why wouldn't I believe you?"

"I know what you're thinking."

"Really? Okay then, what do vegan zombies eat?"

"What are you talking about?"

"A vegan zombie, what's he eat? You know what I'm thinking, so what's the answer?"

"Don't make fun of me."

"He eats grrraaaiiinnnns," Joe howls, grabbing Emily and nibbling on her neck. She laughs and calls him an idiot.

He sets the alarm on his phone for five thirty and lies down for a nap before his shift at the bar. Emily sits beside him, reading *Anna Karenina*, and the sound of the pages turning shortly becomes the crackle of flames in a funky dream of fire.

Mitchell's back in his usual spot at the bar, bitching about a new movie he saw that was a rip-off of an older, better one and acting like Wednesday's brawl never happened. Baba's back too. He's bleached his bowl cut and jokes he's going K-pop.

They're slammed from happy hour on. Joe doesn't take a break until after ten, and then only long enough to eat some tacos from a truck parked out front and suck down a smoke. He sticks to Diet Coke when he's behind the bar, wants to be sharp for the meeting with Danny.

The big excitement of the night is a girl finding some false teeth on the dance floor. She brings them to the bar wrapped in a Kleenex. They unnerve Joe, the garish pink gums reminding him of something he saw at the bridge at Nasiriyah.

"Those yours, Pops?" Baba asks him.

"If anybody comes for them, they're under the register," Joe says.

A short time later a guy in his mid-thirties wearing the Stetson everyone's wearing these days motions Joe over and asks if anybody turned in any dentures.

Joe retrieves the teeth, still wrapped in the Kleenex.

"Can you prove they're yours?" he says.

The guy lifts his upper lip to show bare gums before realizing Joe's fucking with him. "Let me have a double well bourbon in a rocks glass," he says.

When Joe sets the drink in front of him, the guy swirls the dentures in the booze, dries them with a napkin, and pops them into place. Then he downs the bourbon.

"That one's on me," Joe says.

Toward closing, when things slow down and he has time to think, he gets nervous. You heard all these stories about Danny, how he did time for murder, how he's mixed up with La Eme. And it was only a week ago that the dude treated him like a straight-up punk when he tried introducing Baba to him. He has to go into this meeting hard. He has to forget his manners and put on his prison face, put on his war face.

★ ★ ★

Taco Taco is pumping. Joe has to park two long blocks away on a dark street of fortified warehouses and spooky homeless camps. The bag of dope won't get past the pat-down at the entrance to the club, so he leaves it and the pistol in the truck's toolbox. A rat scurries across his path as he's walking over and sets his heart to pounding in time to the bass beats that pass through the club's cinderblock walls to rattle nearby car windows.

The big vato doorman sends him to the end of the line tonight instead of letting him in. He'd text Danny to tell him he's there but is afraid of coming off as desperate. It's after three when he finally makes it inside. The music's so loud, it feels like someone's punching him in the chest. He bumps into somebody while his eyes are adjusting to the gloom and gets an elbow and a dirty look.

There's no sign of Danny in the main room, so he moves into the second. Noisy winners and even noisier losers crowd around the craps and blackjack tables. Danny's playing one of the slot machines. He gambles automatically, emotionlessly, barely glancing at the screen. The two gangsters with him, the young one tall and thin with a pockmarked face and Rams jersey, the older one short and fat with a goatee and droopy mustache, are just as stoic.

Joe tightens up and approaches the trio.

"Dude," he says to Danny.

Danny glances at him, then turns his dead-eyed gaze back to the screen. "Joe Hustle," he says. "You want me to meet more of your friends?"

"I've got something I'm looking to unload. I thought I'd let you have first crack at it."

"What could you have that I'd want?"

Joe leans in close. "Heroin. Looks like half an ounce."

"Where'd you get a half ounce of heroin?"

"What do you care?" Joe says.

Danny locks eyes with him. Joe stares right back, giving as good as he's getting.

"Where is it?" Danny says.

"Let's take a walk," Joe says.

Danny smirks. "Joe Hustle wants to take a walk," he says to his homies.

Joe leads them out of the club. When they turn onto the street where the F-150 is parked, a homeless dude is kicking a tent and screaming at the top of his lungs. Another guy dances around with a burning road flare in his hand. Danny stops short. "Where the fuck we going?" he says.

"You scared of the dark?" Joe says.

"Don't even play," Danny growls.

The bums are still screaming and dancing when they reach the truck. Joe unlocks the toolbox and takes out the heroin.

"Give it to Beto," Danny says, jerking his head toward the skinny vato.

Joe hands over the bag. Beto pulls a butterfly knife from his pocket and flips it open. He sticks the blade into the bag and scoops a bit of powder onto the tip. Lifting the blade to his nose, he snorts the dope, a blast in each nostril. Everybody stands there and watches him swallow hard. After fifteen seconds or so, he smacks his lips and says, "It's legit."

"How much you want for it?" Danny asks Joe.

"A thousand bucks," Joe says. "It's worth double that."

"Not to me," Danny says.

He reaches into his pocket for his roll, peels off a few bills, and holds them out.

"Here's three hundred," he says.

"Fuck that noise," Joe says.

"You better take it, 'cause I'm taking the dope."

"What do you mean? You're ripping me off?"

"Ain't nobody ripping nobody off. Right here's your money."

"No deal," Joe says. He moves to grab the bag from Beto, but the dude brings up his knife.

"See, now you pissed me off, so you don't get nothing," Danny says. He sticks the money in his pocket, and he and his homies walk away.

Let it go, Joe thinks, but as he's thinking it, he's reaching into the toolbox. He pulls out the Glock and points it at the gangsters.

"Gimme the dope," he says.

Danny scoffs at him, says, "You trying to die tonight, fool?"

Joe aims at his head but lowers the barrel before pulling the trigger. The round strikes sparks as it bounces off the asphalt at Danny's feet, the shot barely audible over the noise from the club. Danny yells and clutches his leg. A fragment of the bullet must have struck his shin. Beto, still with the dope, and the other guy run off. Danny limps after them. Joe tracks him with the pistol but doesn't fire again.

The bums are staring at Joe. He locks the gun in the toolbox, jumps into the truck, and speeds away before Danny and his crew come back strapped.

July 20, 11:26 p.m.

All these posters. Do you collect them?

Kind of.

Is there money in it?

A 1931 *Dracula* sold for half a mil.

No shit? What's the most valuable one you've got?

Probably that *Lost Boys*. I could get maybe three hundred for it.

Three hundred? That's all? I guess I won't be breaking in later.

That's not funny.

I'm not a thief.

I don't know that.

Now you do.

Because you say so?

I hate thieves. My dad was a thief.

So maybe it's in your blood.

Dude, *I'm* the one that gets ripped off. Where I live, they steal the tires off your car, they steal the mail, they steal your Christmas decorations. I don't steal because I know what it feels like to work for something and have some lowlife come along and take it. That makes me a chump in the eyes of some people—*you* might even think I'm a chump—but fuck you, and fuck them.

14: HOSTILES

Joe pulls over as soon as he's sure he's in the clear, wipes the Glock, and tosses it down a storm drain. He can't believe he was such an idiot. Yeah, the house burned down, but he was able to get his stuff and has a little money left and a job where he can make more, so there was no need to try to pull off a half-assed drug deal with an animal like Danny, a stunt that's put him in much deeper shit than he was before. Because now Danny will be looking for payback, and he knows he can find him at the bar, which means just showing up for his next shift could be dangerous.

The bleakness of his situation exhausts him. He can barely drag himself from the garage of the Comfort Inn to the room. Luckily, Emily's out cold, not even stirring as he downs two beers in the bathroom and climbs into bed with her. For the second night in a row the sun's coming up before he dozes off.

It's barely eight when he's awakened by the sound of the

shower. Emily emerges from the bathroom wrapped in a towel, shiny and smelling of soap.

"How'd work go?" she asks.

"Same old same old," he says.

"What time did you get back?"

"Late. There was some after-hours thing in the VIP room."

Emily's in a rush to get back to Los Feliz. It's one of the kids' birthdays, and she promised to help set up for the party. So things must be better between her and her sister. Good. Joe goes down to the breakfast room with her. An Asian family is at the table next to theirs, what looks like a band on tour at another. Emily has Froot Loops, a banana, and two chocolate doughnuts. All Joe wants is coffee.

"Let me treat you to one more night here," Emily says.

"No need," Joe says. "A buddy of mine has an extra room."

"But I want to hang out with you."

Joe digs his thumbnail into his Styrofoam cup, working up the nerve to say what he has to say next. What comes out when he's sufficiently steeled is "Listen, I'm in a little trouble."

"What kind of trouble?" Emily says.

"Dirtbag shit. I fucked up."

"You won't tell me what it is?"

"No. It's too stupid. But it's better we don't see each other until I get clear of it."

"That doesn't sound stupid, it sounds serious."

"I don't know if it is or not. I'm still figuring things out. And until I do, it's better to be safe than sorry."

Emily pauses. Her jaw tenses. "Are you dumping me?" she says.

"Come on," Joe says.

"Because I don't feel like I'm being dumped."

"You're not being dumped. I fucking love you."

"You fucking love me?"

"I fucking love you."

Emily taps her plastic spoon on the table and points it at Joe. "Can we talk on the phone?" she asks him.

"Yeah, sure," he says. "And everything'll be back to normal soon."

He walks her to her car. Before she climbs inside, she says, "Be careful, Joe."

"Don't worry about me," he says. "I can wiggle out of anything." He wishes he was as sure of himself as he sounds. It's impossible that Danny knows where he is right now, but he nonetheless keeps looking over his shoulder. There's no way he'll be able to get back to sleep, so he goes ahead and checks out of the room.

He drives around while prioritizing. First thing first: How to deal with Danny? The bastard wasn't hurt too bad if he was able to run away, but he'll still regard Joe taking a shot at him as a major affront. It'd be a mistake to roll over and beg for forgiveness, however. Fuckers like Danny despise weakness and take advantage of it whenever they sense it. Joe doesn't want to end up under his thumb, so he stays hard, texting him, *You owe me, motherfucker.*

The next thing is finding somewhere to crash. Sleeping in the truck is an option, but Keith could call for it at any time. So who owes him a favor? Greg Mollin owes him a favor. They've known each other since third grade, and a few years ago Joe saved his ass. The dude had borrowed five grand from a bookie who rode with the Vagos and was behind on his payments. The bookie caught up to him one night when he was drinking at McRed's, where Joe worked at the time. Mollin was about to lose some teeth or worse until Joe took the money to settle the debt out of the bar's safe and handed it over to the bookie. Mollin got the dough back to him the next day, so the bar's owner was never the wiser.

Mollin started out doing fine. His dad owned a sandwich shop, and when he dropped dead of a heart attack at forty-five, Mollin took over the business. He got married, had a couple kids, and bought a house in North Hollywood. Joe didn't see him much during this time and got the feeling Mollin was avoiding him. He remembers running into him once back then, and all the guy talked about was craft beer and a boat he wanted to buy.

Soon after that, though, he fucked everything up. Besides hoppy IPAs, he also had a thing for titty bars, and got caught cheating with a girl who danced at one. The judge gave his wife the house, the kids, and half the sandwich shop, and he returned to his childhood home in Burbank, moving in with his mom. He and his wife sold the shop a year later, couldn't work together, and Mollin used his share of the proceeds to buy a limo, the first in a planned fleet.

This is where he was at—living with his mom, driving the limo, and spending his nights at McRed's—when Joe loaned him the money. Since then his mom died, leaving him the house, and he totaled the limo with a blood-alcohol content twice the legal limit. Now he day-trades away the money he earns as manager of a Subway. Once again, he and Joe don't see each other, but these days it's Joe who avoids him. The guy has excuses for every mistake he's made, and there's nothing more irritating than a blow-it who refuses to acknowledge blowing it.

Mollin's so happy to hear from him when he calls, Joe gets the feeling he's not the only person avoiding him. Joe tells him about the fire, and even though it's been two years since they last spoke, he invites Joe to stay at his place without him even having to bring up the bookie.

"It'll probably be just two or three days," Joe says.

"Long as you want," Mollin says.

His house in Burbank is around the corner from the one Joe lived in as a kid. Joe drives past that house and sees it's been torn down and replaced with condos. No big deal. A lot of shitty stuff happened there. In fact, they can tear down the whole neighborhood for all he cares.

Mollin's place looks exactly like it did in the nineties. Same weedy yard, same badly patched stucco, same faux-wrought-iron aluminum porch rails. Joe pauses to glance down at the words SLAYER and JUDAS PRIEST etched into the sidewalk in front of the house. He and Mollin, fourteen years old and tripping balls on mushrooms, left their mark when the walk was repoured after sewer work.

"It's still there," Mollin calls from the porch. "And I'm still grounded for life."

Mollin hasn't changed or updated anything inside the house, either, except for the TV. A sixty-five-inch Samsung faces the same recliners Joe recalls from when they were kids, though now the black leather has split and is held together by duct tape. There's an Xbox too.

"You into gaming?" Mollin asks.

"Not really," Joe replies.

"Stay here long enough and you will be," Mollin says.

He's dressed in camo cargo shorts and a wrinkled pink Izod and clutches a bottle of beer. He was a skinny kid, but he's fat now, sloppy fat, with a big round pumpkin head. The fringe of hair he has left hangs over his ears, a black Dodgers cap hiding his baldness on top.

He leads Joe back to a bedroom with a set of bunk beds. There are posters of surfers and skateboarders on the walls.

"My boys stay here when they sleep over, but they don't come around much anymore," he says. "Brock starts college in the fall. UCSD. Got a water polo scholarship."

Joe sets his backpack on the bottom bunk.

"Want a beer?" Mollin says.

"Sure," Joe says.

They walk to the kitchen, and Mollin takes a bottle out of the refrigerator, opens it, and pours the beer into a pint glass.

"This is your standard pils, but they do a nice job with it," he says.

Joe sips the beer and says, "It's good." They stand there listening to a fly buzz over the dirty dishes in the sink. Mollin swats at it but misses.

"Your house burned down?" he says.

"The house I was living at, yeah," Joe says.

"What happened?"

"No idea. I just woke up and ran."

"You know who's a firefighter? Remember Brian Durkin?"

"Spud?" Joe says.

"Fucking Spud," Mollin says. "I saw him at Casa Vega a while ago." His phone dings. He squints to read a text. "Hot tip," he says. "I've been killing it playing the market lately. My Tesla's up five grand. You into stocks?"

"Nah, man," Joe says. "It's been hard times lately."

"I've been there," Mollin says. "Hey, can I get you to help me with something?"

They walk out into the backyard through the sliding glass door. Mollin kicks a pile of dried dogshit off the patio and into a flower bed.

"The boys have a dog they bring with them," he says. "They're supposed to clean up after it."

The swimming pool in which he and Joe spent many a lazy, stoned afternoon is empty, the bottom blanketed with a stinking sludge of decaying leaves, palm fronds, and beer cans. A mylar balloon—HAPPY BIRTHDAY—bounces weakly against the stained wall of the deep end, on its last legs.

Mollin wants to move a bench and set of weights from the garage onto the patio. He plans to start working out. "I'm going Paleo too," he says. "Cutting carbs." He and Joe carry the bench together, then make multiple trips to bring out the plates and bar. Mollin is huffing and puffing when they finish. Still, he sets the bar on the bench's cradles and loads it with plates.

"I could bench two fifty when I was twenty-three," he says. "What about you?"

"I don't know," Joe says. "I was lifting pretty regularly in the Marines."

"And in prison, right?" Mollin says.

Joe's bugged that the guy's thinking about him in prison, but he lets it go, saying, "Nah. Too much drama around the pit."

Mollin motions to the bench. "You first, playa."

"Not now," Joe says.

"Show me what you got," Mollin says. "It's only a hundred and forty pounds."

Joe lies on the bench, grips the bar, and pumps it three times, the last lift slow and shaky.

"That's enough," he says.

Mollin lowers himself onto the bench. He presses the bar smoothly once, struggles the second time, and barely gets it into the cradles on the third.

"Put ten more on each side," he says, breathing hard.

"You're gonna fuck yourself up," Joe says.

"Spot me."

Joe adds the weight and stands at the head of the bench. Mollin lowers the bar to his chest. Puffing his cheeks and blowing out air through pursed lips, he pushes hard but only manages to raise the load halfway before faltering. Joe takes hold of the bar and pulls it up into the cradles just as the guy's arms are about to fail.

"I'll be back up to two fifty in no time," Mollin says. "Should be no problem with all the extra body weight I've got now."

Joe goes out to buy groceries. Bread, peanut butter, eggs, chili. Mollin's refrigerator contains mostly beer and leftover takeout. With great ceremony, he clears a shelf for Joe and assigns him his own cupboard. Joe heats a can of soup, makes a sandwich, and watches Mollin play a war game on his Xbox.

"This village is full of hostiles," Mollin says as a soldier on the TV screen dives for cover behind a wall. "They look exactly like the villagers, so you have to figure out who's who." The soldier kicks open a door, enters a room, and comes upon a woman in a burka. She reaches for something, and the soldier shoots her dead, blood spattering. Turns out she was picking up a baby.

"You get penalized for that," Mollin says, "but sometimes it's fun as shit to blast everyone."

Joe wishes he could drop him into Suicide Alley and watch him fall apart.

When Danny hasn't responded to his text by five, Joe convinces himself the guy is content with having ripped him off and is going to let the shooting slide. He decides to risk showing up for his shift at the bar. The Dodgers are in San

Francisco, but it's still a busy Sunday, with people coming in to watch the game on TV. Joe's slammed from the moment he steps behind the stick, drinkers three deep. Around eight his phone chirps. He checks it and finds a text from Danny: *Look up motherfucker.* He spots him and the two vatos who were with him at the club in the booth near the front door. They snuck in without him noticing.

Danny grins, makes a finger pistol, and mimes squeezing off a shot. Joe goes as cold as a corpse. Keeping his face blank, he takes a couple of empty glasses to the sink, where Manuel's doing dishes.

"Meet me on the patio," he says to him.

"*Qué pasa?*" Manuel says.

"I need you to do me a favor."

Manuel dries his hands and ducks under the flap to get out from behind the bar. Joe waits until he's out the back door before grabbing the bar's keys and going under the flap himself. He weaves through the crowd as nonchalantly but as quickly as possible.

The patio's packed with people laughing and shouting at one another. Joe motions for Manuel to follow and walks to the gate in the ten-foot steel fence that seals off the opening of the alley, all the while keeping an eye out for Danny. He unlocks the gate, opens it, and hands the keys to Manuel.

"Hurry and lock up behind me," he says, and runs for the parking lot. He starts the F-150 and almost backs into Shannon's Volvo in his haste to get away, then makes a reckless right into traffic on Sunset, cutting off a bus.

His phone blows up on the 101. First, it's Baba texting, *Where the fuck r u?,* then it's Shannon calling. Next, he gets a text from Danny: *See you soon.* So that's that. He can't return to the Shorty, not if he wants to avoid a showdown with the gangster. All that effort talking his way back into the best job he's had in years, and he's fucked it up again. At least he's safe at Mollin's. Nobody in the world knows he's holed up there.

He stops at Wienerschnitzel for chili dogs and hits a liquor store for a pint of Jack, a Coke, and a pack of Marlboros. He'll beat the shit out of Mollin if he has to watch him play at killing hajis again, so he stops instead at Izay Park, where he hung out as a kid. Sitting on the bleachers overlooking one of the baseball diamonds, he drinks half the Coke and refills the bottle with whiskey.

The orange glow of the sodium vapor lamps takes him back. Every corner of the park holds a memory. There's the tree he fell out of and broke his arm, there's the trash can where he found a stack of bondage magazines that blew his mind, there's the picnic table he was lying on when he had a vision of death that still haunts him. And now here he is again, twenty-five years later, a grown man with no job and no place to live. Pathetic.

He's pouring more Jack into the Coke when a text comes from Emily: *I miss you.*

I'll call tomorrow, he texts back.

A flashlight beam shines in his eyes. A security guard's standing at the bottom of the bleachers.

"The park's closed," the guard says.

"You used to be able to hang here all night," Joe says.

"Not anymore," the guard says. "Six a.m. to ten p.m."

Joe can tell the guy isn't going to move until he leaves. "That's fucked up," he says, standing and starting down the bleachers. "I got my first blow job here."

He thinks he's back in prison when he comes awake the next morning looking up at the bottom of the bunk above him. He walks into the living room, where Mollin's lying in the recliner where he left him watching *Deadliest Catch* when he went to bed last night. He's watching Fox News now.

Joe scrambles some eggs and makes toast. He's going to stop by McRed's today and see if they're hiring. The place has a different owner now, and it's a sports bar instead of a dead-end dive, but maybe his history there will give him a leg up.

Mollin asks if he wants to hit the weights, but Joe tells him he's got too much going on. Mollin walks out to the patio by himself and does biceps curls. Joe's phone rings. It's Keith.

"What's up, dude," Joe says.

"Who's this?" a woman's voice asks.

"Who's this?" Joe replies.

"This is Jennifer, Keith Swanson's wife."

"Oh, hey, this is Joe McDonald."

"Did you hear what happened?" the woman says.

"What do you mean?" Joe says.

"Keith's dead."

Joe's ears ring like a gun's gone off next to his head. "What?" he says.

"He OD'd and got put in jail," the woman says. "And as soon as he got out, he overdosed again and died."

July 20, 11:28 p.m.

I've been working since I was fourteen.

What kind of job can you get when you're fourteen?

I was a parking-lot attendant at a restaurant where my mom worked. I handed out tickets when people pulled in and made sure the tickets were stamped when they left. It was minimum wage, but I was living at home, so it was enough for everything I needed. Sneakers, weed, McDonald's. I was saving for a car too. After six months, though, my mom got fired because she wouldn't fuck the owner of the place, and they fired me the same day. I got another job a week later, cleaning up construction sites. I bagged groceries at a supermarket, worked at Baskin Robbins, worked at a car wash. You never had a job when you were a kid?

I worked at a movie theater in college.

A movie theater. I've been working continuously except for when I was in the Marines. Two jobs at a time, three. Even when I was locked up, I worked. As a cook.

Where are you working now?

I just got canned from a bartending gig, so I've been taking whatever I can get. Painting, construction. I need a car. I bought a VW last month, sold the truck I had to get the money, and it blew up a week later. I'm thinking about suing the chick that sold it to me. Do you know any attorneys?

My brother's an attorney.

Hook me up with him. Will he do a contingency thing? Although, is it even worth it for two grand? I think I'm fucked on that. Do you have any food? I'm starving.

15: HAPPY HOUR

Keith's wife is calling Joe because calls were made to his number from Keith's phone in the days before he died, and she wonders if Joe knows anything about what happened to him. He doesn't tell her about Keith asking him to score for him or the call from the hospital. He says all they ever talked about was work. He waits for her to mention the truck. She never does, so he doesn't either. His life will be a lot easier if he can hold on to it for a few more days, until he gets a vehicle of his own.

"I'm sorry," he says at the end of the call, remembering the story Keith told him about his son, the Little League player.

"Me too," Keith's wife says.

Joe shuts down after this. He feels like there's a veil between him and the world around him, like his eyes are windows he's looking out of instead of part of his body. It's something that happens when too much comes at him at once. The shrink the

Corps made him talk to after Nasiriyah called it *dissociation*. He'd be okay if he could crawl back into bed for the rest of the day and give his brain time to catch up, but here's fucking Mollin wanting to go to breakfast, wanting to lift weights, saying, "Play this game with me, dude, show me how a real killer does it," so he grabs his keys and phone and flees.

An hour later he finds himself in front of the Town Center Mall. He parks the truck, goes inside, and wanders through Sears, Macy's, a shoe store. On the ground floor is a little train ride for kids that goes round and round on a miniature track. This holds his attention for a while. A big stuffed bear is slumped in the locomotive. He's supposed to be driving but looks like he's drunk.

Joe asks the girl in the theater ticket booth which movie starts next. It's a superhero thing, but not a superhero he's heard of. He buys a ticket anyway. There are only three other people in the theater, and Joe's asleep before the commercials have finished. He wakes once to see the hero fighting the villain in New York, tossing taxis and buses and crashing through skyscrapers, and again at the end, during the final throwdown on the moon.

He orders three fish tacos and a Pacifico from a Mexican place in the mall's food court. The beer's gone in no time, so he orders another. He'd like to keep drinking but has too much to do. He looks up McRed's on his phone and discovers it's now called the Scoreboard. He figures he'll swing by later, after he shaves and changes clothes. Next, he texts Grady and some other car guys, asking if they know anybody selling something cheap.

His lighter dies on him when he steps outside to smoke and call Shannon. It takes five tries before he finds someone with a match. He tells Shannon he's sorry about disappearing last night but had a personal emergency. Why didn't he let her know at the time? she asks. He thinks about how she fucked him over on the VW and how he had to kiss her ass afterward in order to be rehired. "Are you pissed because me leaving meant you actually had to work?" he asks her. She sputters a reply, but he cuts her off, telling her that he won't be back, it's none of her business why, and they can hold his last check until he has a new address. "Whatever, dude," she says.

Grady calls as he's walking back to the truck through the parking structure. His neighbor has a 2002 Civic he'll let go for $1,200. Joe doesn't have that much but heads over anyway, thinking he can talk the guy down or work out payments. Before he even makes it to the freeway, though, Emily calls. He almost lets it go to voice mail but remembers he promised to touch base with her today. He can tell she's crying before she even says, "You have to come and get me."

"What's wrong?" he asks, his mind flashing to Danny, that he's somehow tracked her down.

"My sister's kicking me out," she says. "I know you're dealing with your own shit, but I don't have anyone else to call. I need your help."

It seems like every time he comes up with a plan to get back on track lately, a bomb goes off. "Not now," he wants to say, but instead tells her he's on his way. The sun's shining right into his eyes. He reaches for his sunglasses and realizes, god-fuckingdammit, he left them on the table at the taco place.

He expects Emily to be in front of her sister's house when he arrives, but she's nowhere to be seen and doesn't answer her phone. He gets out of the truck and walks down the side of the house toward the backyard, wondering if he ought to be sneaking. The warm breeze gusts. Leaves rattle, doors slam, and a wind chime jangles with the urgency of a burglar alarm, but the angry shouts of Emily and her sister arguing on the patio drown it all out.

"Give me the keys."

"I let you use the car on the condition that you follow my rules. You're not following them, so no more car."

"You call that helping me? You call that supporting me?"

"That's insulting. I've been nothing *but* supportive."

"You treat me like a child. *That's* insulting."

The sister notices Joe standing there. "What are you doing on my property?" she says.

"I asked him to come get me," Emily says.

"You're the guy who was working here last week," the sister says.

"I fixed the fence in back," Joe says.

"Don't talk to her," Emily says. She grabs the handle of a red rolling suitcase. "Let's go."

"Did she tell you she's severely bipolar?" the sister says. "Did she tell you she just got out of a hospital?"

"He knows," Emily says.

"Did she tell you she stopped taking her meds? Against the advice of her doctor?"

"The doctor who's being paid by her," Emily says. "The doctor who'll say anything to keep getting paid by her."

"You're not helping her by taking her away from here," the sister says. "You're getting in way over your head."

"Maybe a break would do you both some good," Joe says.

"You don't know what the fuck you're talking about."

Another blast of wind flips a chair into the pool and rips a dreamcatcher off the wall.

"Come on," Emily says. "Let's go."

"If you leave, you can't come back," the sister says.

"Ooooh, tough love," Emily says and sets off down the side of the house. One of her suitcase wheels hits a bump, and the case topples over. Instead of pausing to right it, she drags it on its side until Joe catches up, lifts it by its handle, and carries it the rest of the way. He puts it in the back seat when they reach the truck.

"She said she was going to have me locked up again," Emily says. "I didn't know what else to do."

"It's fine," Joe says. "Let's go somewhere and figure things out."

"I need a drink."

Joe drives to Ye Rustic Inn in Los Feliz, a bar that serves food in case Emily wants to eat too. It's dark inside, cool, quiet, made for day drinking. They slide into a big curved booth with room to spread out. Emily orders a tall gin and tonic, Joe has a beer. He talks her into a basket of fried zucchini.

Her eyes look tired, but she's abuzz with nervous energy, some part of her—fingers, knees, lips—always in motion.

"What set her off?" Joe asks, meaning the sister.

"I don't want to talk about her," Emily says. "She already takes up too much space in my brain. Let's talk about you. Have things gotten any better?"

"They haven't gotten worse."

"Did I fuck up your day?"

"I was going out to look at a car."

"What kind?"

"A hooptie," Joe says. "Know what that is?"

"Dude," Emily says, pretending to be insulted he asked.

"It's all I can afford right now," he says. "I'm gonna be changing jobs too, looks like."

The waitress delivers the zucchini. Emily dips a spear in ranch dressing and bites into it, then grimaces and spits the bite into a napkin. "Hot!" she says.

"Slow down."

They order another round of drinks. The booze and food settle Emily some, and Joe's feeling better too. He starts to enjoy being here with Emily and listening to her story about some guy who tried to roofie her at a club but was so obvious that she switched glasses so he got the dose instead. Joe likes watching her face while she talks. There's always something new to see. And her laugh, how it gets away from her sometimes. He'd act the fool with no shame to hear her laugh.

"Now you," she says. "You tell a story."

"Okay," he says. He's sipping his third beer and thinking about getting a shot to go with it. "It's a club story too. A buddy of mine got ahold of a police badge, and we took it to this dance place in North Hollywood where it was Eighties Night or some shit. The bartender pointed out a dude that dealt coke there, and me and Nolan, my buddy, cornered the guy in the bathroom, stuck the badge in his face, and took his drugs."

"That's insane," Emily says.

"Yeah, but of course karma kicked in. Nolan got so fucked up he crashed his car into a bus bench later that night, and we ended up booking, leaving the car and the coke behind."

"Is that the kind of trouble you're in now?" Emily says.

Joe doesn't want to answer, doesn't want her to know he's as dumb now as he was then. "Nah," he says. "That was a long time ago."

Emily orders wings and more drinks, a shot for him. He tells her he's not sure he has enough cash to cover it.

"I got it, I got it," she says, pulling a Visa card out of her wallet. "We're a team now."

They smoke a joint on the patio, and time gets loosey-goosey. Emily talks about making movies, how she always shoots more stuff than she needs because sometimes a shot she's goofing around on turns out to be the key that unlocks the whole film. Nobody's ever talked to Joe like this before. "I feel like I'm getting smarter just from hanging around you," he tells her.

The happy hour crowd drifts in, the TVs go on, a baseball game, and the first song of the day, "Santeria" by Sublime, thumps out of the jukebox. Joe bobs his head to it while talking to a couple of DWP guys splitting a pitcher after work.

"That's a good job, isn't it?" he says. "Union and shit."

"Yeah, yeah," the one guy says.

"Will they hire someone with a felony on his record?"

"I'm pretty sure."

"How do I apply?" Joe says.

"It's all online," the guy says. "Google it."

This makes the other guy laugh.

"And you'll give me a recommendation?" Joe says. "Let me use you as a reference?"

"Yeah, sure," the first guy says. "Tell them Jose sent you."

The other guy laughs again. Joe laughs too. They think they're fucking with him, but he's fucking with them. He doesn't want to work for the DWP.

Emily's getting deep about UFOs and vortexes in Joshua Tree with a jewelry designer and her boyfriend, both of whom are drunk. Joe feels like he's behind a bar, eavesdropping on customers, and this makes him think about the Shorty, something he *doesn't* want to think about right now, so he ducks outside for a cigarette, bumping into someone on the way, then someone else. Excuse me, excuse me. The sun's going down—he and Emily have been here that long. A girl he met last time he was here or the time before keeps looking over even though she's with another guy.

"I remember you," Joe calls to her.

"What?" she says.

"Carol. Carly, Carol."

"Wrong person."

"Really?" Joe says.

He's sure it's the same girl. Seventy-five percent. But even if he's mistaken, she could be nice about it.

"You're pissed I never called you, aren't you?" he says.

"Stop," the guy she's with warns.

Joe flicks his cigarette butt at them and goes back inside.

It's gotten louder. Six people are crammed into booths meant for four, and two rows of standers are waiting to order at the bar. Joe has to turn sideways to get back to where Emily is. The jewelry designer and her date have been replaced by four new people. They scoot closer together so Joe can squeeze in. He's sweating but doesn't have anything to wipe his face with.

"This is Joe," Emily announces. "My Lord and Savior."

"Have a shot," a guy with a bushy red beard says. He hands Joe a glass from a tray in the center of the table. "It's called a Tootsie Roll."

Kahlúa and orange juice. Drinking for Dummies. Joe downs it and turns to Emily, hoping she'll turn to him and say, "Let's get the fuck out of here," but she's talking about TV with some girl, so Joe pretends to watch the game.

A song comes on, "Bitch Better Have My Money," and Emily grabs her new friend's hand and shouts, "Dance party!" Joe stands so they can slide out, and they cut loose in the narrow space between the bar and the booths, weaving like dueling cobras.

"No dancing!" the tattooed blond bartender shouts.

"Come on," Emily whines.

"No fucking dancing!"

Emily's partner raises her hands in surrender, but Emily blows a kiss and keeps moving.

"I'll throw your ass out," the bartender warns. Emily flips her off with both middle fingers. She hurries to the flap. Joe wraps his arm around Emily, but she stiffens and pulls away.

"Fuck her," Joe says. "Let's split."

"I'm not afraid of her," Emily says.

"Come on, get your stuff. We'll go somewhere else."

She retrieves her purse, and Joe rushes her past the bartender, who's waiting near the door.

"Buh-bye," the bartender says. "And don't come back."

Emily plants her feet and twists to reply, but Joe keeps pushing. Her anger cools once they reach the parking lot. "Oh, my god, it's nighttime," she says, pointing at the bright, just-risen moon.

"We put in a full shift," Joe says.

"Kiss me," she says.

Joe puts his lips to hers. She thrusts her tongue into his mouth and squeezes his cock. When they come up for air, he says, "What's your plan?"

"Take me to the motel," Emily says. "I'll stay there tonight."

"Don't waste your money," Joe says. "Come to my place."

"Don't lecture me," Emily says. She's putting on lipstick. It's not going well.

"I'm not lecturing you," Joe says. "Just for tonight, crash with me."

Emily draws back and looks him up and down. "You said you were in trouble," she says.

"I'm in the Valley," Joe says. "The Valley's safe."

Emily laughs like this is the funniest thing she's ever heard.

★ ★ ★

Joe's drunker than he thought. He has to squint to see straight a few times during the drive to Mollin's house. Mollin is sitting in his recliner watching MMA when they come in. He's still wearing his Subway shirt and Subway hat. He gives Joe a look that makes Joe think he should have warned him Emily was coming but stands to greet her and offers her a beer.

"I've been drinking gin," she says. "Do you have any gin?"

"No gin," Mollin says. "Tequila?"

"No! No tequila. A beer'll be fine."

"IPA or pilsner?"

"You choose."

Joe sits on the couch beside Emily. She puts her head on his shoulder.

"Me and this dude have known each other since we were five," Mollin says from the kitchen.

"Was he a *Star Wars* kid?" Emily says.

"Ha!" Mollin says. "Not exactly."

"How's he changed?"

"He didn't have tattoos back then."

Mollin brings Emily the beer, poured into a glass.

"Where did you guys meet?" he asks her.

"In church," Emily says.

"Ha!" Mollin says again. "Are there other women as cute as you at this church? Just kidding."

Emily asks about the house. Mollin relates the history of it as proudly as an earl or a duke discussing his family's ancestral manor. He rhapsodizes about how great the neighborhood was to grow up in, everyone going all out to decorate for holidays, baseball games in the street, kids mobbing the ice cream truck on summer afternoons.

"It was the best time of my life," he says.

Joe was there for all of that, but it means nothing to him, less than nothing.

When Emily goes into the bathroom, Mollin whispers, "Is she sleeping over?"

"Just tonight," Joe says. "She got kicked out of where she was staying."

"I'm cool with you being here," Mollin says, "but I don't want a bunch of strangers hanging around."

"It was an emergency."

"Getting laid is an emergency?"

"I'm serious, man."

"Okay. Shit happens. Tonight's fine, but now you know the rules, right?"

The guy talking to him like he's lecturing one of his kids makes Joe want to slap the smirk off his face, but all he does is say "Thanks, buddy."

Emily looks askance at the bunk beds.

"I've been sleeping on the bottom," Joe says. "But you can have whichever you like."

"I'll squeeze in with you," Emily says.

The only way that works is for her to turn her back to Joe and him to hug her, both of them lying on their side.

"A coffin built for two," she says. "How romantic."

Joe slips his dick inside her for a quick, quiet fuck. Immediately afterward he's asleep, his batteries exhausted. The bed's shaking when he wakes two hours later, still half drunk. *Earthquake,* he thinks, but, no, it's Emily crying.

"What is it?" he asks.

"I want to see my daughter," she says.

"So go see her," Joe says. His arm underneath Emily is asleep, completely numb. He has a hard time rolling her over to face him.

"Will you drive me?" she says.

"To Austin?"

"I'll pay for gas, for hotels. Will you take me to see Phoebe?"

It's three thirty in the morning. Joe's ready to say whatever it takes to settle her mind and let him get back to sleep and stave off his hangover for a few more hours.

"Sure," he assures her. "No problem."

"Thank you," she says, "thank you," kissing him on the cheeks, the nose, the lips while he makes a fist and tries to force blood into his tingling fingers.

July 31, 1:04 a.m.

Was prison rough?

Was prison rough.

Was it?

Not rough like you're thinking, ass-rape and all that. If you keep your mouth shut and steer clear of psychos, you can do easy time in a place like Chino. But, I mean, you *are* living in a dorm with a hundred other dudes, so that blows.

Sounds disgusting.

It didn't stress me that much. I'd only been out of the Marines for a couple years, so I was used to showering and shitting in front of strangers and sleeping a foot away from snorers. For me, it was a good break from drinking and doping. I worked in the kitchen, and that helped kill time and kept me out of trouble. I read a lot too. *The Forty-Eight Laws of Power,* you ever read it?

Never even heard of it.

Seriously? Law four: Always say less than necessary. Law nine: Win through actions, not arguing. Law forty-eight: Assume formlessness. *The Martian Chronicles* was pretty good too. Ray Bradbury.

Give me some stories I can use though.

About Chino?

Yeah, prison stories.

Prison stories. Okay. Prison stories. There was this old vato named Sleepy who was in for the fifth or sixth time behind some drug thing, a righteous con who kept to himself, didn't hassle anybody, no gang shit, just wanted to do his nickel in peace. He adopted a stray cat that hung around the yard and named it J.Lo. He snuck it food, and it would jump up in his lap and sit there purring while he scratched its ears. Cute, right? But prison's an evil place. If you've got something that makes you happy there, you keep it hidden, otherwise some motherfucker who wants you to be as miserable as he is will fuck it up. Sleepy should've known that, but maybe he thought being an OG got him a pass, or maybe he was just stupid. Whatever it was, he loved that cat right out in the open, and the law of the jungle kicked in. J.Lo turned up with her neck broken. When Sleepy got out to his spot on the yard and saw her laying there, he didn't freak. He just bent to pet her one last time, then turned around and walked back to the dorm. The dipshit who killed the cat—a Black kid, a Crip—joked about it. "Fuck that old-ass Mexican," he said. "I ain't got no pussy, he can't have no pussy." The guards looked the other way when Sleepy cornered him in the shower and gouged his eyes out. The kid lived but got transferred to Vacaville, where they keep blind inmates, and Sleepy ended up at San Quentin with so much time tacked on, he'll for sure die inside.

Poor J.Lo.

I think that's what he called her. That's how I tell it. The story's probably bullshit anyway. The dude who told it to me was a liar ten times over.

You didn't see it for yourself?

Is that a rule? You didn't say anything about that's how it had to be.

16: BARSTOW

Wʜᴀᴛ ᴡᴀᴋᴇs Jᴏᴇ ɪɴ ᴛʜᴇ ᴍᴏʀɴɪɴɢ ɪs Eᴍɪʟʏ sᴄʀᴀᴍʙʟɪɴɢ out of bed to run to the bathroom, where she vomits long and loud, moaning between retches.

"Jesus fucking Christ," Mollin yells from somewhere.

Joe's doing okay himself, not a hundred percent, but nowhere near as rotted as he expected to be. Emily closes the bedroom door when she returns, puts her back to it, and slides to the floor to sit cross-legged with her chin on her chest. Joe remembers his promise to her from last night but hopes she's forgotten asking for it. Her first words, though, are "When are we leaving?"

"Are you sure you're up to it?" Joe says.

"You changed your mind."

"No, but you don't look like you're in any shape for a road trip. Maybe we should chill today and go first thing tomorrow."

Emily gets to her feet and rakes back her hair with her fingers. "I'll be fine after some coffee," she says. "Worry about yourself."

Joe ignores the argument raging in his head. He knows, he knows, he knows it would be a huge mistake to drop everything and drive Emily to Texas right now, when his own life is in shambles. Mollin wants her out of the house, though, so Austin or no Austin, he has to make at least that happen.

Mollin's doing shoulder presses on the patio. Joe goes out to talk to him while Emily gets ready. It's already hot at ten a.m. The trash in the pool stinks.

"Dude, your girl," Mollin says, making a face. "I almost puked myself."

"Five more minutes and we'll be out of here," Joe says.

"Not to be an asshole or anything…"

"It's cool."

Mollin sets the bar down and wipes sweat off his face with his forearm.

"I might be going out of town for a while," Joe says.

"Where to?" Mollin says.

"Austin."

"Right on. Austin's cool."

"I want to thank you for letting me crash here the last few days."

"No problem," Mollin says, extending his fist for a bump. "We've got history."

Emily seems to be feeling better after washing up and brushing her teeth. Joe packs his stuff, and they head out. She's on her phone looking for the nearest Starbucks when they pass a doughnut shop.

"Ooooh, a maple bar," she says. "Pull in there."

They sit at a tiny orange table overlooking the shop's

parking lot. Someone's etched a tag into the window, some nonsense six inches square that warps Joe's view. The coffee's burnt, but his doughnut is excellent.

Emily's on her phone again. She turns it around to show Joe a map. "It's twenty-two hours to Austin," she says.

He knows, he knows, he knows this is his last chance to get out of the trip. Instead, he uses two fingers to enlarge the map and says, "All the way on the 10, huh?" He was serious when he told her he loved her the other day, and now he guesses he'll prove it.

"Yeah, but we've got to swing through Vegas," Emily says. "One night, have a little fun."

The last time Joe was in Vegas was for that fucked-up Christmas at his mom's, which was no fun at all.

"And the Grand Canyon, too," Emily says. "I've never been there."

Neither has Joe, but he wonders when this turned into a sightseeing trip. "You're not in a hurry to get to Texas?" he says.

"We have to stop anyway."

Joe sips his coffee. The Asian lady who sold them the doughnuts slips out from behind the counter to wipe the tables. Joe remembers coming here as a kid. An old white guy owned the place then, always said "God bless you" when he handed you your change.

Their next stop is a gas station. Emily goes into the store while Joe fills the truck. He pops the hood to check the oil and coolant. A homeless man offers to wash the windshield. Joe tells him to go for it. Skinny Black dude, crusty jeans hanging off him, dead leaves in his hair. He does a decent job, though, even using newspaper to get rid of the streaks from the squeegee.

"Watch out for the fire," he says.

"What fire?" Joe says.

"In the mountains."

Joe looks north toward the hills, follows them east. Smoke smudges the sky in the distance.

Emily comes out of the store with a tube of Pringles and a six-pack of Heineken.

"Provisions," she says.

Joe digs in his pocket for a couple bucks to give the window washer. All he has are twenties.

"How about a beer?" he asks the guy.

"Sure," the guy says.

Joe takes one of the Heinekens and hands it to him.

The quickest route to Vegas, according to Emily's phone, is the 5 to the 14 to the 138, picking up the 15 in Victorville. They breeze through Santa Clarita, but traffic slows and backs up after that. The problem turns out to be the fire. The dry, scrubby hills north of the freeway are ablaze, and the truck crawls bumper to bumper toward a towering plume of peach-colored smoke. When everything eventually comes to a dead stop, Joe turns on the radio and finds a news station. He and Emily sit there, feeling trapped and antsy, listening to a reporter talk about a brush fire off the 14.

"Someone doesn't want us to leave," Emily says.

Three fire trucks race past in the breakdown lane, and a few minutes later traffic begins to move, everyone inching along again, creeping closer and closer to the blaze. Joe glimpses flames up ahead. His eyes sting from the smoke in the air, and delicate flakes of ash whirl like snow and cling to the truck's hood. Emily's recording the apocalyptic scene on her phone. She turns the lens on Joe and asks, "Are you scared?"

"Are you?" he replies.

A huge plane flies so low over the truck, Joe can count the rivets on its belly. It drops a load of bright red retardant onto the fire, which is now only a quarter mile in front of them. Before they reach it, flares, orange plastic cones, and gesticulating highway patrol officers force the F-150 and all the other vehicles off the freeway at the Acton exit.

It's stop-and-go on the subsequent detour down frontage routes and back roads. The truck is stuck in a line of vehicles that stretches as far as Joe can see in both directions, and it takes half an hour to go five miles. Joe's hangover finally hits, and Emily's energy flags too. She sinks into sullenness, turning off the radio and staring blankly out the windshield. Joe can't think of anything to say and doesn't try. They creep along in tense silence.

A set of rubber bull balls dangles from the trailer hitch of the truck in front of them. The driver of the Jeep behind them is playing a game on his phone. Joe watches in the rearview mirror as the guy purses his lips in concentration, thumbs tapping wildly. Emily suddenly comes back to life. She scrabbles for the six-pack and tears a can off it.

"Do you want one?" she asks him.

They're sipping their second cans when they're allowed back onto the freeway outside Palmdale, and soon they're speeding across the desert toward Victorville. There's no feeling of relief though. It's ugly, barren country dotted with ugly little clusters of decrepit mobile homes and scorched stucco ranchers haunted by paroled child molesters and deranged end-timers who wound up here after being run off from everywhere else.

The beer's gone by the time they reach Barstow, and Emily has to pee. She points out a McDonald's and says there's good, she'll get something to eat too. The trek across the parking lot is like walking on a hot skillet. They pass an empty bus and find the passengers, Chinese tourists clutching outlet mall shopping bags, lined up at every register inside the restaurant. Their guide shouts instructions, pointing out the soda fountain, the restrooms, the seating area.

"What do you want?" Joe asks Emily. "I'll order while you go."

He's still in line when she returns from the bathroom, so she grabs a table. He has the order memorized, but his mind goes blank when he finally reaches the counter. The cashier fidgets impatiently while he stutters and stammers and squints at the menu, struggling to get everything straight again.

He carries the tray to where Emily is sitting. Her head's on the table, her cheek resting on the backs of her hands.

"Rise and shine," he says, his own head pounding.

Emily sits up, bleary-eyed. "Wow," she says. "I'm wiped out. Maybe there was something toxic in that smoke."

Joe hands her a box of McNuggets. "These'll set you right," he says. "You didn't say what sauce, so I got honey mustard and barbecue."

Everyone else in the dining room is Chinese. Joe decides they must be on their way *to* Vegas instead of coming back because they're in too good a mood to have just spent a few days losing their asses. A young woman at the next table unwraps an old woman's hamburger, cuts it in half with a plastic knife, and sets it in front of her. At another table a kid uses his phone to film himself slurping a shake.

Joe works on his Big Mac and fries. He's not hungry but feels like he should get something in his stomach besides a doughnut. Thinking his headache might stem from dehydration, he twice refills his cup with Coke. Emily eats only three of her nuggets before making a face and closing the box.

"Do you want something else?" he asks her. "Ice cream?"

"I've got to go to the bathroom again," she says. "I think I'm gonna vomit."

Joe tells her to meet him outside when she's done. He has a cigarette under a jacaranda tree in the parking lot, sharing the shade with three of the Chinese tourists, who are also smoking. The sky's a flat, featureless white that makes him feel like he's trapped inside an eggshell. Emily approaches, pale and projecting discomfort.

"I should have listened to you earlier," she says. "I'll die if I have to sit in that truck any longer. Let's get a room here and start fresh tomorrow."

They check in to the first motel they come to, a Super 8 next to the freeway. Their room's on the second floor, overlooking an Indian medical clinic, then a bunch of railroad tracks, then desert. It smells like weed and deodorizer, and the fake wood flooring is curling up in one corner, but Emily says, "Fuck it," and falls onto the bed.

Joe gets a bottle of Tylenol out of his kit bag and swallows three capsules with a glass of nasty tap water. He's exhausted but doesn't think he can sleep.

"I'm gonna get some beer," he tells Emily. "Do you want anything?"

"Please don't bring back any alcohol," she says. "I know I'll end up drinking, and I don't want any more today."

"Okay. Fine," Joe says.

"Some Perrier would be good though, or any kind of sparkling water."

Hoping to tire himself out, Joe walks instead of drives to a supermarket they passed on the way in. He regrets it after one block, with the heat and the dust and the semis rattling like they're about to fall apart as they lumber toward the freeway. He's the only fool on foot except for a tiny Latino, a child or a dwarf, crouched in the thin strip of shade cast by a power pole. A cloud of flies lifts off a dead cat in the gutter, and Joe breathes through his mouth as he hurries past it.

A wave of cold air breaks over him, a welcome shock, when the doors slide open at Von's. He gets a cart and walks the aisles until he cools down. Emily might be on the wagon tonight, but he's going to want some beer, so in addition to two bottles of Perrier, he picks up a twelve of Bud Light and a bag of ice. There's a cooler in the truck's toolbox. He'll stash the beer there and slip out of the room when he feels like having one.

On his way back to the motel he spots a bar that shares a crumbling parking lot with a Dollar General and a Little Caesars. OPEN 6 A.M., a sign says, HAPPY HOUR ALL DAY! It's so dark inside, he has to pause to let his eyes adjust. The girl pouring drinks is a stone speed-freak: bony, scabby, twitchy. She hits a pen and exhales a cloud of cherry-scented smoke before asking Joe what he'll have.

"A draft Bud sounds good," he says.

"Does it?" the girl replies.

When she sets the glass in front of him, he asks if it's okay to smoke.

"Okay for me, but not for you," she says. He can't tell if she's serious but doesn't want to give her the satisfaction of making him ask, so leaves his cigarettes in his pocket.

The only other customer is a bald, buff Black guy playing strip poker on a machine at the end of the bar. "This is some bullshit right here," he says to the bartender. "It cost me ten bucks to see this bitch's titties."

"You coulda seen mine for five," the bartender says, and cackles like an old witch.

Joe downs his beer quickly. He's almost finished when someone enters from outside, riding a blinding bolt of sunlight. There's ten feet of stick on either side of Joe, but the guy stands next to him so close, Joe can feel the heat coming off his body.

"Baby, baby, baby," he says to the bartender. "Let me get a Bushmills on the rocks." He's a postman, a long-haired, pony-tailed, goateed postman. He shuffles his feet, squints at the floor, and backs away.

"Dude," he says to Joe. "Did you piss yourself?"

Joe looks down to see a puddle under his stool. "That's ice, man, melting," he says. "There must be a hole in the bag." He stands and lifts the dripping sack to show everyone.

"Get that shit out of here," the bartender says.

Back at the motel Joe puts the ice and beer in the cooler and locks the cooler in the toolbox. The room's freezing, the air conditioner working itself to death. Emily has undressed and is lying under the blanket and spread.

"You want a glass of this?" Joe asks her, holding up the Perrier.

"Give me the bottle," she says.

She scoots away from him when he crawls into bed. "No touching," she says. "I'm still super nauseous." He rolls over so he's facing away from her and falls asleep listening to the bathroom faucet drip.

He wakes at sunset and sneaks out for a smoke and a beer on the tailgate of the F-150. The heat's broken, and it's pleasantly breezy in the lengthening shadow of the motel. Folks are standing outside their rooms on the second floor, forearms resting on the walkway railing, gazing out at the desert gone purple and pink and orange in the distance and the deepening blue of the sky. Two Black girls have dragged out a chair, and one sits in it looking at her phone while the other braids her hair. They're playing music and at one point start singing along to a song together before dissolving into laughter.

"You sounded great," an old cowboy walking a pair of ancient poodles calls out to them.

Emily's sitting up in bed, watching TV, when Joe returns. She's ready to eat, so they walk to a Panda Express on the other side of the freeway. They pause on the overpass to watch traffic zoom by below, headlights and taillights coming and going, a faint orange glow to the west, the first stars shining brightly.

The fluorescent lights in the restaurant make the travelers wolfing down two-item combos look like they're all about to die. Joe and Emily order orange chicken, beef with broccoli, and fried rice and take it back to the motel to eat at the table in their room. Emily climbs back into bed afterward, but Joe's wide awake, still on bartender time. He goes down to the truck, where he guzzles one beer and grabs another and sets off for the train tracks behind the Indian clinic. He walks along a chain-link fence meant to keep people off the rails until he comes to a spot where someone's cut a hole. It's tight, but he squeezes through and climbs the raised track bed.

Four pairs of rails run here. Two have long strings of well cars double-stacked with containers parked on them. Joe tosses a rock at a container to hear it clang, then climbs a ladder to sit between two of the cars. The metal against his back is still warm from the sun. He writes *JOE HUSTLE* in the grit caked on the nearest container and imagines someone seeing it while unloading the box in China or Africa.

An approaching locomotive sounds its horn. Joe hops down and sees it coming slowly up the outside track, running west, its headlight showing all the dust in the air. He lays a penny on one of the rails and backs off to watch the train pass. It takes a while to get to where he's standing. He waves at the engineer, who blows the horn again in response. What follows is a five-minute parade of military vehicles—Abrams tanks, MRAPs, Strykers—riding on flat cars en route to who knows where. Pendleton, Twentynine Palms, Afghanistan. Joe's mind chants *Motherfuckers motherfuckers motherfuckers* in time to the click-clack of the cars' wheels on the rails. He drains his beer and hurls the can at a passing Bradley. He snatches up a rock and throws that, too.

"Hey!" a fat security guard yells from fifty yards away, waddling toward him with a flashlight. Joe hurries back to the hole in the fence and makes his escape, but without the flattened penny he'd planned to present to Emily as a souvenir.

July 12, 11:55 p.m.

Maslow's pyramid?

Yeah.

I think I've heard of it.

You went to college, didn't you?

I said I think I've heard of it.

This psychologist, Maslow, came up with this pyramid—
well, more like a ladder. Give me a pen, I'll draw it.
Down here on the first level are the basics: food, water,
shelter. On the second level are financial security and
personal safety. Next level, here, you've got relation-
ships: your friends and family, your wife or girlfriend.
Then we come to level four, your esteem needs, when
you feel good about your accomplishments and you're
satisfied with yourself. At the top, up here, the tip of
the pyramid, is self-actualization. That's where you realize your full potential as a human being. Now, the
deal is, you start at the bottom of the pyramid and
work your way up. You have to satisfy your needs at
each level in order to free up the mental space that'll
allow you to advance to the next level, and if you skip
any levels, you'll never attain true self-actualization.

I guess that makes sense.

It makes sense. But my problem is, I'm stuck on level one.
I'm forty years old and still scraping for pennies, still
worried about where my next meal's coming from and
where I'm gonna live from month to month. That
wears you down. It stunts you. Maslow said, "What a
man can be, he must be," but what if *this* is all I can be?

17: BRIGHT LIGHT CITY

Emily points her phone at Joe. "Sing it," she says.

"Stop," Joe replies.

"Don't you want to be in my film?"

Emily woke up feeling fine this morning after a solid night of sleep, and her new thing is she's going to make a movie about their trip. She filmed Joe carrying their bags down to the truck, filmed some teenagers throwing a Frisbee in the motel parking lot, filmed their breakfast at Denny's. Their waitress was a talkative old woman who let Emily shoot her telling the story of how she met her husband.

"He was playing pool in this bar," she said. "I thought he was a cutie, so I walked over and introduced myself, but he flat-out ignored me. I was so mortified, I left. A week later I was at the same place, and there he was again, but this time he bought me a drink. What was going on before was there was a hundred dollars riding on that pool game, and he thought the guy he was playing was trying to distract him by sending me over. I forgave him for being rude, and we've been together ever since."

Now Emily wants to film Joe. They're driving down the Vegas Strip, just got into town, and she thinks it'd be funny if he sang "Viva Las Vegas."

"I don't know it," he says.

"You do too," she says. "Everyone knows 'Viva Las Vegas.'"

He humors her, happy she's happy, Elvis-crooning the chorus as they pass Luxor and Excalibur and New York-New York. The hotels and casinos are nothing special at noon without their lights. The pitiless sun fingers every flaw and worn spot on the older joints—the bird shit streaking the black pyramid, the cracks in the castle's parapets—and makes the new glass towers look like office buildings.

And then there are the ticky-tacky souvenir shops and fast food outlets. The thermometer on the truck's dash reads 103 degrees, and the tourists trudging down the sidewalk are wondering why the hell they left their air-conditioned rooms to spend fifty bucks on a Tango Mango daiquiri and a pair of flip-flops at Margaritaville and close to a hundred on candy and T-shirts and other crap at the M&M's store.

Rooms at even the best hotels are dirt cheap on a Wednesday in the middle of summer. Emily calls the Flamingo and books one for forty dollars. Joe drops her off to check in while he parks the truck. He brings his backpack and her bag to the lobby, his pulse quickening as soon as he hears the electronic bloops and beeps and snatches of music coming from the slots. He's lost a hundred times more in these places than he's won, but the thrill of a good run on a table is still like no other, that hour or so when fortune finally—*finally!*—smiles on him.

The floor-to-ceiling windows of their deluxe king overlook

the Strip. Emily wants to go down to the pool, so they change into their bathing suits. The first pool they come to is like an outdoor club, with booming music and hyped-up people dancing and downing shots. Emily hurries past it, muttering, "No, no, no." The second pool's quieter, the crowd mostly older folks and families. Joe and Emily pick up towels and find two empty chaises in the shade, where the heat's blunted by a hissing mister.

A waitress in a pink vinyl bikini asks if they want anything. Emily orders lemonade, Joe gets a beer. He's in a good mood, and not even the noisy kids roughhousing in the pool can ruin it. He fingers the scab on his jellyfish sting. The wound's healing nicely.

Emily goes to the bathroom and comes back smelling like weed. She pulls *Anna Karenina* out of her bag and lies back on her chaise.

"Hey," she says.

"What?" Joe says.

"Thank you."

"For what?"

"For everything."

"You're welcome."

Joe gets up and walks down the stairs into the shallow end of the pool. The water's too warm to be refreshing, but it gets cooler as he moves toward the deep end, dodging cannon-balling ten-year-olds. When the coast is clear, he holds his breath and dives down to skim along the bottom, his belly brushing concrete, until he comes to the wall. It's not far, twenty feet or so, but he's sucking wind when he breaks the surface. Fucking cigarettes.

He rests his elbows on the lip of the pool and kicks his legs in a semblance of exercise, all the while side-staring at a waitress whose enormous fake tits strain her bikini top. The constant squawking coming from the hotel's wildlife exhibit—ratty parrots, a flock of sun-struck flamingos, koi lazing in a luke-warm pond—almost drowns out the music from the other pool.

Emily's still reading when he gets back to their spot. She's lying on her stomach, knees bent, the pale bottoms of her feet showing. He stands over her and shakes his head, showering her with drops from his wet hair.

"Stop!" she says. "Listen to this." She reads to him from her book, her finger following the lines.

" 'The sight of his brother and the proximity of death renewed in Levin's soul that feeling of horror at the inscruta-bility and, with that, the nearness and inevitability of death, which had seized him on that autumn evening when his brother had come for a visit. The feeling was now stronger than before; he felt even less capable than before of under-standing the meaning of death, and its inevitability appeared still more horrible to him; but now, thanks to his wife's near-ness, the feeling did not drive him to despair: In spite of death, he felt the necessity to live and to love. He felt that love saved him from despair and that under the threat of despair this love was becoming still stronger and purer.'

"That's us," Emily says. "Under threat of despair our love grows stronger."

"What are you talking about, 'despair'?" Joe says. "Every-thing's fine."

"The world is out to get us, baby."

"The world doesn't give a shit about us, and that's a fact."

Emily laughs. "You've got things all figured out, haven't you?" she says.

"Close enough," Joe says, and leans over to kiss her shoulder.

While she takes a dip, he checks his messages. There's one

from Grady about another car for sale, and one from Nolan offering him a few days' work clearing a lot his parents own in Encino. He texts them both that he's out of town.

He has no desire to talk to his mom but knows he'll feel guilty later if he doesn't call her.

"Guess where I am?" he says when she answers.

"Jail?" she says.

"I'm at the Flamingo," he says. "Me and a friend are on our way to Austin, and I thought I'd check in with you."

"That's so sweet," she says, sarcastic.

"Are you at work?"

"I'm on break."

"If I come by and play on your table, will you flash your hole card?"

"You'd still fucking lose. I'll tell you what I will do though: Be at the casino at five when I get off, and I'll buy you dinner at the Chinese place here. It's the best in town."

"I don't know."

"You don't know about a free meal?"

"I don't know if I've got time."

"That's bullshit. Are you coming or not?"

When Emily finishes swimming, Joe tells her about his mom, that she lives here and that he kind of should stop by and see her.

"Can I come?" Emily says.

"You don't want to do that," Joe says.

"What are you worried about? That she won't like me?"

"She doesn't like anybody. She's a fucking bitch."

Emily crunches an ice cube from her lemonade and says, "Then you definitely need me there."

"What for?" Joe says.

"Protection," Emily says.

★ ★ ★

She films as they drive to the Gold Coast, gets a homeless man pushing a shopping cart past a pair of photo hustlers dressed as showgirls, a dude on a freeway overpass holding a sign that reads YOUR ALL GOING TO HELL, and a tumbleweed blowing across Flamingo Road. Joe's always amazed at how ugly Vegas is as soon as you leave the Strip, miles and miles of generic shopping centers, mini-malls, and industrial parks.

"What's your mom's name?" Emily says. She put on a dress for the meeting. Joe told her shorts were fine, but she insisted.

"Her name's Ruth," Joe says.

"And what's Ruth *really* like?" Emily says.

"Our neighbors had a dog that wouldn't stop barking. Mom got her boyfriend at the time to steal it, and nobody ever saw it again. She told me she and her boyfriend took it to the pound, and I said I didn't believe her, that I thought they'd killed it. She slapped me and told me never to say that again. I never did, but I still think they killed it."

"You're fucking with me," Emily says.

"Okay," Joe replies with a shrug.

The Gold Coast is an older casino a mile west of the Strip. It caters to Asian gamblers with lots of pai gow poker and baccarat tables. Ruth's waiting in the restaurant. Joe didn't tell her he was bringing Emily, but if she's pissed about the surprise, she doesn't show it. All she says, fingering the name tag pinned to her gold dealer's shirt, is "You should have warned me. I'd have changed clothes."

"I made him let me come along," Emily says. "I wanted to meet you."

"I can only imagine the stories he's been telling you," Ruth says.

"We're still getting to know each other, so we're keeping it light," Emily says.

Joe's impressed. She's a good liar, knows the right ones to tell to put people at ease without coming across as a phony.

Once they're seated, Ruth opens her menu and asks what sounds good to them, then ignores their suggestions and orders wonton soup, shrimp fried rice, and some sort of noodles. She keeps up a steady stream of featherweight chitchat as polished as an old comedy routine. It's her way of preventing the conversation from straying anywhere she doesn't want it to. Joe's fine with letting her skate through the meal like this, because the last thing he wants is for the two of them to start slinging shit in front of Emily.

Emily's onto Ruth, too, but cheerfully plays along, commiserating with her about her overly strict neighborhood HOA and her hatred of self-checkout at the supermarket, and complimenting her on the new 'do her hairdresser talked her into, a two-tone silver-and-black shag with choppy bangs.

"I got it cut like this when I was fifteen, only in pink," Ruth says. "My mom almost disowned me."

"Well, she can't say anything about it now, can she?" Emily says.

"She sure can't," Ruth says. "She's dead."

"Oh, shit," Emily says.

"Don't worry," Ruth says. "I'm not the sensitive type."

Joe stays out of the conversation, pretending to be absorbed in his meal, but Ruth eventually turns her attention to him.

"How's the new job going?" she says.

"It's going great," he says.

"Have you thought about moving here?"

"I've thought about it."

"I can tell when he's lying," Ruth says to Emily. "I was only sixteen when I had him, so we were more like sister and brother than mother and son."

We were nothing, Joe thinks. *We're still nothing.*

"I can see how that would be," Emily says.

"Do you have any kids?" Ruth asks her.

"One," Emily says. "A girl, Phoebe. She's eight."

"And where is she while you're running around with him?" Ruth says, tilting her head toward Joe.

Emily's smile stays the same, but her eyes change. Joe tenses up.

"She's living with her dad for now," Emily says. "Joe's taking me to visit her."

Ruth also noticed the shift in Emily's energy, Joe can tell, but she doesn't back off.

"What was it? Drugs?" she says.

"What do you mean?" Emily says.

"Is drugs why your husband got custody?"

"Jesus fucking Christ," Joe says.

"It's a question anybody would ask," Ruth says.

"No, it isn't."

"It was my decision that she stay with him," Emily says. "I had some issues, and I felt like it would be better for her to be with him while I dealt with them."

"I didn't have that luxury," Ruth says. "Raising Joe was all on me. I wasn't perfect, but I did the best I could."

"The best you could," Joe scoffs.

Emily lays a hand on his forearm. "Stop," she says.

"He can't," Ruth says. "He's got no self-control."

"You too," Emily says. "Stop it. Come on."

"You come on. Why are you with him anyway? Is one of your *issues* that you have a thing for losers?"

Lost in a red rage, Joe leaps to his feet and flips his plate, showering Ruth with rice and noodles.

"You fucking maniac," Ruth screeches.

"Take it easy," someone yells. The hostess grabs a phone off her desk.

"Let's go," Emily says to Joe.

They make it across the casino and through the door to the parking structure before security can get its act together. Joe breathes deeply, in through his nose and out through his mouth, as they ride the elevator up to the truck. Emily massages her temples with her fingertips.

"Wow, wow, wow," she says.

"I'm sorry," Joe says.

"That was fucking gross."

The elevator doors open, and the two of them walk toward the F-150. Joe notices someone standing on the driver's side of the truck, between it and the car parked next to it, someone trying not to be seen. He immediately thinks *Danny* and sticks his arm out to stop Emily.

"What?" she says.

He shushes her with a finger to his lips and cranes his neck to see what the guy's doing. Turns out he's taking a piss, the stream slithering out from between the truck and the car and racing down the driveway.

"What the fuck!" Joe shouts.

The pisser, startled, fumbles with his zipper and steps out of his hiding place. It's an old Asian man in khakis, a polo, and a Ping visor.

"Sorry," he says in thickly accented English. "Bad kidney. Bad kidney." He backs away with his hands in the air.

Angry at Ruth, angry at Danny, angry at himself, Joe

charges the guy and shoves him. The old man stumbles and almost falls before turning and running away.

"You pig," Joe yells after him, the words echoing throughout the cavernous parking structure.

"Hey, Joe, no," Emily says.

Joe, already ashamed, composes himself before turning to face her. He'd hoped she'd never see him snap.

"Let's go back to our place," he says.

They listen to the radio instead of talking during the drive. Joe's relieved that Emily seems to be willing to let what just happened lie for the moment. At the Flamingo, they sit in front of video poker machines at a casino bar, and Joe explains that you get free drinks while playing them.

"But I don't know how," Emily says.

"Do you know poker? The hands?" Joe says.

"Like a straight, a full house? Sure."

"So you're good to go."

He coaches her through a few hands until she gets the hang of it, then lights a cigarette, sips his complimentary whiskey and Coke, and plays his own machine. He's dealt four spades, holds them, and draws a fifth for a flush. Three hands later he hits a full house. Before he finishes his smoke, he's doubled his money.

"I've got a loose one," he tells Emily, who's already down to five dollars.

"I suck at gambling," she says. "And this drink is all ice."

"Can we get two shots of bourbon?" Joe asks the bartender.

When the drinks come, Emily lifts hers for a toast.

"To Ruth," she says.

"Fuck that," Joe says. "To us."

They touch glasses.

"I've got to tell you, seeing you like that scared me," Emily says.

"I'm fine with her riding me," Joe says, "but I lost it when she went after you."

"*Are* you a maniac, like she said?"

"No, I'm not a maniac."

"Good," Emily says, "because I'm psycho enough for the both of us, and two psychos is too many."

Joe's glad she's back to joking around but wonders if it's an act, if inside she's frightened of him now. If so, it's another thing he'll never forgive Ruth for.

Emily wants to walk down the Strip. The sun has set, but it's still hot. All the tourists are in shorts and T-shirts. Emily pulls a joint from her purse, and she and Joe smoke it in an alley. The weed hits Joe right, muting the noise in his head and bringing a smile to his face. They stop at a booze slushie stand, and he spends most of his winnings on two margaritas in tall pink souvenir glasses. He feels like a fool carrying his down the sidewalk, but the icy mix of frozen limeade and shitty tequila is delicious. Emily takes a sip of hers and touches her cold green tongue to his.

They sit on a bench in front of Paris casino and stare up at the Eiffel Tower for a while. Emily says it's as good as the real one. Inside the casino, the ceiling is painted to look like the sky at dusk, complete with pink-tinged clouds. Emily lies on the floor to film it.

"Is she drunk?" a drunk woman in a cardboard tiara asks Joe.

"She's an artist," Joe says. "Working on a project."

Emily sees a Willy Wonka slot machine and has to play it. She hits a bonus for sixty dollars and marches to the cashier's cage, singing the Oompa Loompa song. They cross the street to watch the Bellagio fountains spurt and sway in sync with "Fly Me to the Moon," then walk through Caesar's. Emily's flagging when they get to the Venetian. Joe suggests they blow her slot windfall on a gondola ride, but she wants to go to bed.

They finish the joint on the way back to the Flamingo. It's not even eleven, and Joe's not ready to call it a night. He takes Emily up to the room and tells her he's going back down for a nightcap and a smoke.

"Here," she says, handing him her winnings. "Turn this into a million."

It doesn't work out like that. He drops some of the money playing video poker at the bar for a free beer and most of the rest at a blackjack table where, because the dealer's flirting with him, he makes the fatal mistake of not getting up after losing three hands in a row. Then, feeling like a sucker, he behaves like one, sticking his last ten bucks into another Willy Wonka slot and pressing SPIN over and over until those fucking Oompa Loompas bleed him dry.

July 22, 11:59 p.m.

I thought about going to college. My grades sucked, but I could've gotten in somewhere. I wanted to study engineering because I always used to come up with ideas for inventions.

Like what?

One thing I remember was a tool to get weeds out of cracks in a driveway. I'd draw up plans and shit. My friend's brother was a plumber, though, and he was only five years older than us and already had a truck and a condo. I looked at him and was like, Fuck college, I'm gonna be a plumber.

What happened to that?

I got caught up in too much bullshit. A guy actually took me on as an apprentice after I got out of the Marines, but he dumped me after a week because I was too much of a drunk. I should have tried again later when I kind of got my shit together, but, you know, time flies when you're having fun. I don't dwell on it though. That's not healthy.

18: OVER THE EDGE

They're packed up, checked out, and on the road by ten the next morning, fueled by breakfast burritos from the casino snack bar and watery Bloody Marys. It'll be a four-hour drive across the desert to the Grand Canyon, the next stop on Emily's itinerary, but Joe's happy to be getting out of Vegas. He locks it in at eighty on the long, straight stretches of highway, marveling when other vehicles blow by him doing a hundred or more.

Emily gets bored filming the barren moonscapes, dried-up towns, and desperate tourist traps they're flying past and instead tries to play the game from *Anna Karenina,* wanting Joe to deduce her messages with only the first letters of the words to go on. "This is impossible," he says after a few unsuccessful attempts. "I'm gonna crash the truck, thinking so hard." They switch the game to hangman, and he does okay at that.

A country station is all they can get on the radio. They take turns fake-singing along, inventing lyrics about goin' to the bar on Friday, Little League on Saturday, and church on Sunday. Seligman, where they stop to piss and stretch their legs, is a collection of gift shops, gas stations, and restaurants catering to people driving what's left of Route 66. They buy dipped cones from an old burger stand and sit at a picnic table in the shade of a corrugated steel awning.

Emily strikes up a conversation with a French family at another table, starting out in French but changing to English when she can't keep up. The family—dad, mom, two kids— is driving across the country in a rented RV, next stop Vegas.

"I like your tattoos," the dad says to Joe, then nods toward his wife. "She only let me have one." He unsnaps the right cuff of his white cowboy shirt and rolls up the sleeve to show Joe the Social Distortion skeleton—hat, cocktail, cigarette— inked on the underside of his forearm.

"I've got that somewhere too," Joe says, and searches his arms until he finds it.

He and Emily go into one of the souvenir stores. Emily pauses in front of every display to finger the key chains, coffee mugs, and T-shirts, looking for something for Phoebe. The warm, stale air of the shop makes Joe dizzy. He sidles up to Emily and says, "I'll wait outside."

Lighting a cigarette, he walks over to a rectangle of shade cast by a sign for the store. Six motorcycles—Japanese bikes ridden by sightseeing Brits—roar into town. The Brits park in front of the hamburger stand, take off their helmets, and unzip their leather jackets.

"I'm as soggy as if I'd had a sauna," one of them bellows.

A commotion at the gas station next door gets Joe's attention. Excited tourists stand in a circle, pointing phones at a bearded desert rat in a filthy tank top, jeans, and liquor store trucker cap. Joe walks over to investigate. What's got everybody worked up is a six-foot rattlesnake pinned under the rat's boot. Someone spotted the snake crawling across the road, and the rat stepped in to take charge. His heel is planted behind the snake's head, and the animal's body whips back and forth, rattle buzzing like a cicada.

"Stay back," the rat cautions the crowd. "If he gets loose, he'll be biting mad."

A father grabs his little girl's shoulder and moves her behind him without taking his eyes off his phone's screen.

"If it bit you, would it kill you?" a boy asks.

"It sure might," the rat replies.

"What'll you do with it?" an old woman asks.

The rat draws a hunting knife out of a sheath on his belt, squats, and calmly cuts off the snake's head with one stroke. The body continues to writhe, and when the rat lifts his boot, it slithers toward the onlookers, prompting some to squeal in fright.

"Did you have to kill it?" a dreadlocked hippy girl asks.

"Out here you don't catch a rattler and then let it go to bite a neighbor," the rat says. He picks up the snake's head and shows it around, pinching the mouth open to display the fangs.

"Careful," he says. "They still got poison in 'em."

After some guy lifts the now-limp body by the rattle and poses for a photo, everyone else clamors to do the same. Joe returns to his shade. He doesn't tell Emily about the snake when she comes out of the store, doesn't want to have to go back over there. She shows him the stuffed bear wearing a Route 66 T-shirt she bought for Phoebe.

"Awesome," he says.

They reach the Grand Canyon around three thirty. Emily gets on her phone while they're waiting in a long line of vehicles to pay the entrance fee and, thanks to a late cancellation, is able to book a room at a lodge on the South Rim at the last minute.

Once inside the park, they drive through more of the same high-desert scrub they've been traversing for the last fifty miles until, all of a sudden, there it is, the canyon, awash in afternoon sun, a fiery gash in the earth, its far rim blurred by dust and distance. Joe doesn't catch more than a glimpse, though. With a car in front of him and another on his ass, he has to keep his eyes on the road.

He pulls off at the first overlook they come to, Mather Point. The parking lot's full of tour buses and RVs, but he wins a standoff with a Prius for a spot. He and Emily get out of the truck and follow a herd of people down a path to the viewpoint, a paved outcropping bounded by a waist-high railing, beyond which is a sheer drop of several thousand feet. They work their way through the crowd to get right up to the edge and take in the panorama of red, orange, and pink rock; vivid green slashes of sagebrush and mesquite; and a bright blue sky hung with a few fat clouds. Stepped and striated flat-topped buttes rise from the canyon floor almost to the height of the rim.

A uniformed ranger shouts factoids over the chatter of the tourists: The canyon was carved out over eons by the relentless current of the Colorado River, which resembles a dirt road winding along the bottom of the chasm. The canyon is a mile deep at its deepest point, eighteen miles wide at its widest, and when you look at its walls with their layers of rock and sediment, what you're seeing is two billion years of geologic history on display.

Joe's disoriented. His senses are having trouble adjusting to the new vastness stretching out before him. He moves away from the edge, scared he might topple over. The dramatic shift in scale hasn't affected Emily. She's shooting long, slow pans of the canyon that end on tourists posing for photos against the overlook's fence.

"I don't feel so great," Joe says when she rejoins him on solid ground.

"Maybe you're dehydrated," she says.

"Maybe so," he says. A hawk soars overhead. Its shadow passes across his face, blocking the sun for an instant, then slides over the ground until it reaches the canyon, where it drops and disappears.

He and Emily get back in the truck and drive to Grand Canyon Village, a cluster of hotels, restaurants, and shops perched on the rim. Their room on the second floor of the Thunderbird Lodge is standard-issue except for the view of the canyon out the window.

They walk to the El Tovar, an old hotel that's a cross between a cabin and a castle, for a drink. Oprah Winfrey stayed here, Emily tells Joe, and Albert Einstein. The taxidermied heads of moose and elk and buffalo stare, dead-eyed, down on the tourists resting on the lobby sofas. The bar's crowded, but Joe and Emily find two empty seats.

The bartender is a girl from Poland who got some sort of contract to come over and work in the park for the summer. She lives in a dorm with other workers from all over the world. Emily keeps her talking while she makes their prickly pear margaritas, thinks her accent is cute. The girl tells a story about a raccoon that steals the workers' shoes at night and another about her roommate, who has ESP.

Emily goes to the bathroom and comes back with a book from the hotel's gift shop. *Over the Edge,* it's called, a collection of accounts of deaths that have occurred in the canyon, everything from falls to hiking mishaps to plane crashes.

"Isn't it sick?" Emily says.

"Not enough pictures," Joe says, being funny.

Emily asks the bartender for a good spot to watch the sunset. She recommends Hopi Point. A shuttle goes there, but Joe and Emily elect to walk the two miles on a paved trail along the canyon's rim. They join a string of hikers that stretches as far as Joe can see in front of and behind them. Daddies herding kids, mommies pushing strollers, old folks on motorized scooters. Joe imagines he's on one of those pilgrimages you see in India or Saudi Arabia, trekking with all these people to some holy spot. Every twenty feet is a photographer crouched behind a long-lensed camera mounted on a tripod. Emily stops now and then, trying to get the perfect shot of them trying to get the perfect shot.

The point is another jam-packed overlook. Joe and Emily continue past it and find a boulder off the path where they can be by themselves. They hit a joint and sit silently, shoulder to shoulder. The canyon changes color constantly as the sun goes down. Joe's fine looking out at it now that he's assimilated its immensity. The buttes and walls darken to purple while the sky blazes orange and yellow and red in wild combinations he's never seen before. He feels like he wants to say something but is too stoned to put words together.

When the sun drops below the horizon, night rushes in to fill the chasm like a flash flood. The air cools quickly, and Joe's acutely aware of the warmth coming off Emily where they're touching. He thinks of it as a kindness. They wait until the first stars appear before starting back to the village.

Fewer people are on the path now, and the rising moon lights the way. Emily takes Joe's hand. He can't remember the last time he held hands with someone. They have another drink in the El Tovar and realize they're starving. You need reservations to get into the hotel's fancy restaurant, and the line is too long at the diner, so they end up in the cafeteria.

Joe has a Navajo taco and a beer, Emily gets a salad with a nasty-looking chicken breast on top. The dining room's full of teenagers on a school trip. Halfway through the meal Joe notices he's doing all the talking while Emily sits silently, poking at her food.

"Do you want something else?" he asks her.

"It's the lights in here," she says. "Fluorescents give me migraines."

They smoke more weed and hang out in the El Tovar lobby, sprawled on a couch in front of a cold stone fireplace. Other tourists are wiling away the evening here too. A family plays UNO at a nearby table, the mother shushing her son over and over for being too loud. Joe trips out on the massive logs that form the walls of the hotel and support its roof. The trees they came from must have been a hundred feet tall.

Emily reads aloud from the "Suicide" chapter of her new book. More people kill themselves at the canyon than at any other national park. Most jump, some shoot themselves, and a couple have driven cars off the edge. A forty-year-old salesman from Phoenix left a last note in his room in one of the lodges before jumping. Another guy was found almost a year after he jumped with a note in his pocket apologizing for making a mess. An employee of the El Tovar clocked out one night, walked outside, and jumped.

On and on it goes until Joe finally tells Emily to stop. Reeling off the details of so many sad ends as casually as if they were baseball stats seems like a sure way to spoil their luck.

"Let's take a walk," he says.

They stroll along the rim until they get away from the lights of the hotel. The sky, heavy with stars, presses down on them. Emily groans and pretends to push back. "It's crushing me," she says.

Coming to a bench, they sit facing the canyon. The chasm is bottomless, the river lost in darkness. If you fell in now, you'd keep falling forever.

"What if my ex moved without telling me?" Emily says.

"You talked to him the other day, didn't you?" Joe says.

"But what if he's taken Phoebe away?"

"You're spinning out," Joe says. "It's the weed."

"*You're* spinning out," Emily says. She relights the joint, takes a big hit, and blows the smoke in Joe's face. Then, suddenly, she's up on the low stone wall that runs between the path and the rim of the canyon, standing with her back to him, staring down into the unfathomable depths. He rises on shaky legs, panic a bony hand tightening around his throat.

"Hey!" he says. "No! Get down!"

"What are you scared of?" Emily says.

"You're high, you could slip," he says. He considers rushing her but is afraid a struggle will send her over the precipice. He moves closer, though, slowly, slowly.

Emily crouches and straightens, crouches and straightens, swinging her arms like she's getting ready to launch herself. "One," she chants. "Two."

"Stop it!" Joe shouts.

"Three!"

She turns and hops off the wall onto the path with a little laugh. Joe grabs her arm. He's shaking not with fear now, but with anger.

"That wasn't fucking funny!" he yells into her face. "That wasn't fucking cute!"

"Oh, come on," she says.

"That's the most fucked-up thing anybody's ever done to me."

"Really?"

Joe squeezes her arm tighter, wanting to get rid of the mean grin on her face. "You're hurting me," she says, and tries to pull away. He drags her back up the path toward the lodge. She resists briefly, then gives in.

"I didn't mean to scare you," she says.

"I should leave your ass here and go back to L.A. right now," he says.

"Do it," she says. "If you're that mad, go ahead."

"Don't fucking tempt me."

She starts to cry. "I thought you loved me," she says.

"Enough, okay?" Joe says. "For fuck's sake, enough."

"Because I love you," she says.

"Shut up."

"I do."

"Shut up!"

Joe doesn't release her until they're in the room, visions of her sprinting for the wall crowding out everything else in his mind.

"Can I take a shower?" she says.

"Do what you want," he says.

He stares at the TV while she's in the bathroom, but if you asked him what was on, he couldn't have told you. He's tormented by the idea that Emily would toy with him just to make him sweat, but even more upsetting is the possibility she was actually contemplating jumping.

She comes out of the bathroom wearing only the Metallica shirt she had on the day he met her. She climbs into bed, turns out the light, and tries to hug him, but he uses his elbow to keep her away.

"Forget it," he says.

She cries again, then falls asleep. Joe lies there listening to her breathe and watching the glow of the TV claw at the walls. After a while he gets up and pulls on his jeans and T-shirt. Slipping out of the room, he walks down the silent hallway to the stairs and down them to the exit. He sits on the wall at the rim of the canyon, but faces the lodge. He can still feel the canyon at his back, though, an open grave beckoning the lonely and the lost.

He's halfway through a cigarette when he notices the mule deer scattered across the swath of lawn between the lodge and the path, fifteen or twenty of them, antlered bucks, does, tiny fawns. They all stop cropping grass to stare at him, their eyes blazing with reflected moonlight, and he gets the crazy notion they're not deer at all, but the spirits of the canyon's suicides conjured by Emily reading from her book earlier. Spooked, he stubs out his smoke and creeps past the animals to return to the lodge, not resting easy until he's in the room with the door locked behind him.

July 15, 1:53 a.m.

I haven't changed since I was fourteen. I knew everything then that I know now. I don't mean the stuff you
learn in school or on a job, I mean the truth of this life,
the no-bullshit truth. But maybe it's like that for everybody. Maybe we all realize the truth at fourteen
and spend the rest of our lives finding ways to forget it
or struggling to keep going carrying the weight of it.
And what is this truth?
You know.
No, I don't.
Yes, you do.

19: ALBACRAZY

Emily's all over Joe, kissing his neck and grinding on his leg, when he wakes up the next morning. It's too soon, after what happened last night.

"Let's just get going," he says.

If Emily is stung by the rejection, she doesn't show it. Changing course smoothly and without comment, she hops out of bed, dresses, and packs her bag. They keep the conversation light during breakfast—how good the pancakes are, whether it's going to be hotter today than yesterday. The only time they veer anywhere near her craziness on the rim of the canyon is when Joe asks how much farther it is to Austin.

"You're still taking me?" Emily says, trying to sound like she's joking when Joe knows she isn't.

"Looks like it, doesn't it?" he says.

He picks up the 40 in Williams and heads east. He and Emily ride mostly in silence, listening to whatever music they can pick up on the radio and staring out at the red desert, blue sky, and towering white clouds. A Willie Nelson song's playing as a cloud shadow slides across a distant mesa. When the shadow has passed, the sun strikes the mesa, turning it bright orange. Emily lays a hand on Joe's leg and nods toward the sight at the exact instant he was about to point it out to her, and Joe considers this the best moment of the trip so far.

They gas up at a truck stop in Gallup and get sandwiches from Subway, which they eat at an outside table that has a view of semis pulling up to the pumps. Joe has to weight down his chip bag with his drink cup to keep the wind from scattering Doritos across the desert. A raven croaks at him from a telephone pole before dropping to the ground to peck at a black patch on the pavement.

A man and woman approach, big people in sweatpants and New Orleans Saints jerseys. The woman, holding up a hot dog and an Arizona Iced Tea, asks if it'd be okay if they sat too. Joe and Emily slide over to give them room. They're a husband-and-wife truck-driving team out of Baton Rouge, real chatterboxes. This is his fourth marriage, her third. They met at a bar but don't drink anymore. The best thing they ever did was sell their house, buy their rig, and hit the road.

The woman pulls up photos of grandchildren on her phone. Joe doesn't even pretend to be interested, but Emily eggs the couple on. Everything's fine until she asks if she can film them.

"What for?" the man says, his grin tightening.

"For a documentary I'm making," Emily says.

"Are you from the media?" the woman says.

"I'm a filmmaker," Emily says.

"We don't want to be in your movie," the man says. "We're Christians."

Joe gets up and goes into the store. It sells everything from

SpaghettiOs to boxer shorts to truck mini-fridges. Joe buys a tall can of Budweiser and downs it in the bathroom. He peruses the rack of mesh ball caps and picks out a red one with an American flag on it. Emily's alone at the table when he returns.

"Where are your friends?" he asks her.

"They had to leave, but they're going to pray for us," she says.

"No, they won't," Joe says.

"Are you really gonna wear that?" Emily says, meaning the hat.

"I'm blending in," Joe says.

Their motel in Albuquerque is across the road from a McDonald's. Joe can hear people ordering from the drive-through whenever the sound of traffic fades. Emily chose the place because it was close to Old Town Plaza, a park and a few adobe buildings that were the heart of the original city. They walk over and find that some kind of festival is taking place there. Carnival rides and games fill the plaza, and mariachis play on the bandstand. The historic church Emily wanted to see is closed for restoration, and it's too late to visit the Rattlesnake Museum, but they wander around for a while, eating churros and snow cones.

The sun's going down, and the heat has eased somewhat when they get back to the motel. Joe buys a twelve-pack, and they drink the beer sitting by the pool. They're too lazy to change into their bathing suits, but Joe takes off his shirt and Emily wades out until the water reaches her jean shorts. A little boy wearing floaties is splashing in the shallow end, surrounded by dusk-pink ripples. "That lady has her clothes on," he whisper-yells to his mother about Emily.

Emily climbs out of the pool and drips across the deck to rejoin Joe. They go back to the room with its groaning air conditioner, stained carpet, and weird painting of a coyote baying at the moon. Emily lies on her stomach on the bed, reading *Anna Karenina*. She's wearing the Metallica T-shirt with nothing on under it again. Joe, watching *Wheel of Fortune,* catches a glimpse of the bottom half of her rear end where the hem of the shirt has ridden up to expose it and gets instantly hard. He rests a hand on one of her ass cheeks, and she gives him a sideways "What are you up to?" look. Ten seconds later they're fucking like teenagers sneaking one in before their parents get home.

"Spit in my mouth," Emily says in the middle of it.

"Seriously?" Joe says.

"Yeah, yeah, come on," she says, opening wide and sticking out her tongue.

Joe does as she asks, but it messes with his concentration and he almost goes soft.

Emily says they've got to have green chile for dinner. She finds a place near the college that people like on Yelp, and they drive over. You order at a counter and wait for your number to be called. They both get burritos.

Emily wants a drink afterward. Joe says sure, but he's prepared to cut her off if he sees things veering anywhere near where they went last night. They try a bar down the street from the restaurant. It's full of college kids doing karaoke, though, so they leave without ordering. On the drive back to the motel, Joe spots a divey cinderblock saloon and points it out.

"Now you're talking," Emily says.

It's a shithole exactly like a million other shitholes. Sticky bar, wobbly stools, warped pool cues. A pair of steer horns and three dusty Stetsons hanging on the wall represent a stab at a "country" theme. The gray-ponytailed bartender doesn't greet them when they sit down. He and the two other customers in the place are watching an MMA bout on a big-screen TV.

"Couple of Buds when you get a chance," Joe says.

Without taking his eyes off the fight, the bartender slides open the cooler, grabs the bottles, and brings them over. Only then does he give Joe a quick, appraising glance that lingers on his truck-stop hat.

"That'll be twelve dollars," he says.

"Twelve dollars?" Joe says. "Can't we get the locals price?"

"It's the same price for everyone," the bartender says.

"That was a joke," Joe says. He hands the guy a ten and a five and tells him to keep the change.

Emily walks around looking at the old video games and the ads posted on the bulletin board. She comes back, sips her beer, and says, "I'm going to apologize once more for last night, and then we won't talk about it again."

"Fine with me," Joe says.

"I get too high sometimes and start acting out the movie in my head."

"I understand," Joe says. "But here's some advice for when that happens: Don't piss off your driver."

"You're not just my driver."

"I hope not."

"You're not."

A woman enters the bar, a skinny Indian with the scabby face and jutting jaw of a tweaker. Her gaze alights briefly on Joe and Emily before she joins the other customers, two guys as rough as she is. A hushed conversation ensues. The guys leave, and the bartender puts on music, loud. The tweaker turns to Joe and Emily and yells, "Where you from?"

"L.A.," Emily yells back, and the tweaker moves down the bar to take the stool next to her.

"I lived in L.A. for a while," the tweaker says. "In Garden Grove."

"Where is that exactly?" Emily asks her.

"I got robbed there," the tweaker says. "I got raped."

"That's terrible," Emily says.

"Albacrazy's no better," the tweaker says. "It's full of assholes." She opens a bottle of pills, shakes two into her hand, and downs them with beer, then begins to babble, jumping from story to story. Something about a job she's getting on a food truck, something about the police following her, something about a gold bar she's going to inherit from her grandpa and how she's the only one who knows where on the reservation it's buried.

After five minutes, Emily turns to Joe and mouths, *Yikes.* "We gotta get going," Joe says.

"Hold on, though, hold on," the tweaker says. "Can you buy me a beer?"

Joe calls for the bartender to bring her another Corona. The dude slow-walks it over and slow-walks the change for the twenty Joe gives him. By then Joe's itching to get out of the place. He and Emily burst through the door like they're being chased.

"Oh, shit," Emily says as they approach the truck. The passenger-side window is broken. Icy blue pebbles of glass are scattered across the seat and glint in the lot's gravel. The glove compartment and center console are open, and the contents of both are strewn about. Joe never noticed what was stored in them so has no idea what's missing besides Emily's sunglasses, which were on the dash.

He goes back inside the bar. The tweaker glances at him, eyes pinwheeling in her head.

"My truck got broken into," Joe shouts over the music.

"You want me to call the cops?" the bartender says.

"Is there a camera on the lot?"

"Nope, no cameras."

"I figured," Joe says.

He's still angry as he vacuums glass off the seat and floor mat at a twenty-four-hour car wash. The way he sees it, the tweaker was stalling them while the scumbags who left the bar broke in. The bartender was in on it too, turning up the music to drown out any noise.

"They probably target tourists," Emily says.

"Fucking buzzards," Joe says. "Fucking cockroaches."

"Those were my favorite sunglasses."

Joe pulls a sheet of cardboard out of the car wash's dumpster and uses a piece of it to replace the window, securing it with duct tape off a roll he finds in the truck's toolbox. Back at the motel, his anger deepens and darkens. Emily drifts off to sleep, but he's seething, drinking beer and staring at home makeover shows on TV while contemplating driving back and beating the shit out of the bartender.

Around midnight he actually gets dressed and steps outside but manages to talk himself down before doing anything stupid. He paces the motel parking lot, smoking and listening to people order from McDonald's, until his jaw unclenches.

July 25, 11:14 p.m.

You look kinda swole. You been working out?

I worked this week pouring a patio, and the dude was too cheap to rent a mixer, so we had to shovel-mix everything in a wheelbarrow. Maybe slinging all that mud got me yoked.

I was gonna challenge you to arm wrestle, but now...

"To be the man, you got to beat the man." Remember Ric Flair?

No.

The wrestler? The Nature Boy? The stylin', profilin', limousine-ridin', jet-flyin', kiss-stealin', wheelin' and dealin' son-of-a-gun?

I was never into wrestling.

When you were a kid? "Whatcha gonna do, brother, when Hulkamania runs wild on you?" I said that to a guy once when we were squared up in this bar, about to go at it, and it threw him long enough for me to get the first punch in.

Do you fight a lot?

Not anymore. Right after I got out of the Marines, though, I fucking loved to fight. It shut off the static like nothing else. But I wasn't a bully. I only fucked with guys that were bigger than me, sometimes two at a time.

That's a good way to get yourself killed.

I don't know. It was harder than you think to get someone pissed off enough to duke it out. I was pretty buff from the service. I'd have to call their girlfriends whores, throw drinks in their faces, spit on them.

Jesus. Did you win at least?

Winning wasn't the point. I just wanted to get hit in the face. Most fights go to the ground after a few punches anyway, and you roll around until someone breaks it up. But that's all in the past. I haven't started shit with anybody in eight or ten years. I must have worked through whatever problem I had back then, right? Ha!

20: ONE MISSISSIPPI, TWO MISSISSIPPI

It's green chile again for breakfast, omelets this time, at a diner on old Route 66. No matter how much coffee Joe drinks, he can't shake the funk he woke in. Worried about the truck, he hardly slept, getting up three times to make sure it was parked in front of the room. His mood darkens even more when, in the middle of his meal, he gets a text from a guy in L.A. about a painting gig, four days' work starting tomorrow, and has to turn the job down.

Emily's messing with her phone, knees bouncing under the table, while the waitress clears their dirty plates. She says something about detouring through Marfa.

"We're going the rest of the way today," Joe says.

"To Austin?" Emily says.

"I'm gonna power through. You can take over if I need a break."

"It's like twelve hours."

"I can do it."

"Are you sick of me?"

"I thought you were dying to see Phoebe," Joe says. "I'm trying to get you there as fast as I can."

"I appreciate that," Emily says, but it seems to Joe she's sulking after this, giving him the silent treatment, which is okay. He doesn't feel like talking either.

She buys new sunglasses at the gas station where he fills up the truck on the way out of town, a pair with big round rainbow-tinted lenses.

"Those are godawful," he says when she comes out wearing them.

"So's your hat," she says.

Once they're on the freeway, the high-desert vistas that were so beguiling yesterday quickly become monotonous. The one station the radio picks up keeps fading in and out, so Joe shuts it off. Emily wants to stream a podcast from her phone, but he says he'd prefer silence. He uses the quiet time to put together a list of what he needs to do when he gets back to L.A. but quickly realizes it's the same list he had before he left—get a car, get a job, find somewhere to live.

The wind picks up with gusts powerful enough to swerve the truck. The cardboard where the window used to be flexes wildly, and Joe's hands ache from his death grip on the steering wheel. A dust storm that's been smudging the northern horizon since they left Albuquerque edges closer and closer to the freeway, finally engulfing it, a swirling orange fog that dims the sun and cuts visibility to just beyond the truck's front bumper.

Traffic slows, and Joe proceeds at a crawl, squinting to keep track of the car in front of them. The truck's headlights go on automatically, but the beams turn the cloud into a wall, so Joe kills them. Snakes made of dust sidewind across the asphalt, and dust fills the gap between the hood and windshield. Emily films for a while before putting down her phone and leaning forward to help watch for brake lights.

The wind's still blowing and the dust's still swirling when they hit the New Mexico/Texas state line. Joe pulls into a truck stop to take a break from wrestling the F-150 and decides to top off the tank while they're there. The card readers at the pumps are out of order, so Emily has to pay inside. Joe goes with her to get out of the wind. A girl is mopping up a dark, syrupy puddle on the floor, yellow safety cones warning customers away. Joe recognizes blood when he sees it. He takes Emily's arm and steers her around the mess. She figures out what the smear is too, and murmurs, "Oh, my god."

"What happened?" she asks the guy who swipes her Visa card.

"A fight," the guy says.

A police car pulls up, and a cop gets out and comes inside.

"Sky Daniels and some other dude went at it, then both took off," the guy tells the cop.

"Whose blood is it?" the cop asks.

"Sky's."

"He get stabbed?"

"Punched in the nose."

Joe was thinking about eating a sausage off the roller, but fuck that now. He gasses up the truck while Emily goes to the bathroom. She returns smelling of weed.

Back on the road, the dust isn't as bad, but the wind hasn't eased a bit. This doesn't faze the other drivers though — even the big rigs are doing eighty again — and Joe has to push the F-150 to sixty-five, faster than feels safe, to keep up with the flow.

The wind doesn't faze Emily, either. She's out cold in no time, legs curled under her body, head resting against the door. She sleeps pretty, mouth closed, no snoring, like she's only resting her eyes.

Thirty miles outside Lubbock, Joe's own lids grow heavy. He blinks, shakes his head, and starts counting cotton fields and cows in an effort to keep himself awake. Grandpa Buck grew up on a farm somewhere out here but joined the navy at seventeen in order to get the hell off it. Farming was nothing but pulling tits and shoveling shit, he used to say.

The next thing Joe knows, Emily's screaming his name. He dozed off and the truck drifted onto the shoulder and is now juddering along with two tires in the dirt. It slams into a mile marker, knocking it over, before Joe manages to steer back onto pavement and come to a stop.

The sun grabs him by the back of the neck when he gets out to check for damage, and the wind almost shoves him into the path of a passing semi. Emily hops down too, and has to hang on to him to keep from being blown away. They stand together in front of the truck, sizing things up. They got off easy with only a dent in the bumper.

"I'm driving," Emily says.

"I'm awake now," Joe says.

"Austin's still six hours away. If you're already falling asleep, what'll happen when it gets dark?"

It's three p.m., and they haven't even had lunch, so Joe says fine, they'll stop in Lubbock for the night. The highway slices right through the city's drab, depressing downtown. All the buildings are the color of dirt and there's no shade anywhere. They eat at Taco Bell and check into a Super 8, get a ground-floor room with a patched but not painted hole in one wall and a door that looks like it was kicked in at some point. The window looks out onto a Phillips station on the other side of the parking lot.

Joe walks to the station's store. A fat goth girl with dyed black hair and face tattoos rings up his beer and cigarettes. Trying to be friendly, he asks her who the most famous person from Lubbock is.

"I don't know," she says. "Buddy Holly? They got a museum about him over on 18th."

Joe wants whiskey, too, but the girl says he'll have to buy it at a liquor store down the street. He returns to the motel instead. Emily's watching a court show. "You know those are fake, don't you?" he says. He tells her about a guy he knew who got paid to be on *Judge Judy* and act like he'd stolen his girlfriend's dog.

When the wind dies and the sun begins to go down, he and Emily move the room's chairs out to the walkway and sit there drinking beer. The parking lot fills with the trucks of construction workers who are also staying at the motel. They tear into thirty packs of Natural Light and gather around tailgates to share pizza from Domino's. Country music pumps out of one of the truck's speakers. A big, bearded dude in a cowboy hat cracks everyone up by doing a silly dance to a white-boy rap about rodeo.

"Bro!" another big bearded dude admonishes. "There's normal people here." He nods toward Joe and Emily.

"Where you guys working?" Joe says.

"Building a wind farm in Hale County," the guy in the hat says.

"Good money?" Joe says.

"All money's good, ain't it?" the guy replies, to guffaws from his friends.

"Where y'all from?" another guy asks.

"California," Joe says. "L.A."

"I'm sorry," the guy quips, to more laughter.

Dinner's in a noisy restaurant across the street from the motel. Joe and Emily smoke a joint before walking over. A softball team is celebrating a victory there, guys in uniforms and their wives and girlfriends and children. Joe's catfish tastes like fried chicken, and Emily's chicken tastes like catfish. A fly keeps buzzing their faces and landing on their food. Joe almost knocks his beer over twice, swatting at it.

"Austin's nicer than this, I promise," Emily says.

She has dark circles under her eyes. It could be the fluorescent lights, or it could be she's feeling what Joe's beginning to feel, the strain of spending so much time with someone you hardly know. Taking a long trip together so soon after meeting probably wasn't the best idea, but then again, it's also a little late for common sense to be kicking in.

Two girls are playing a pattycake game, chanting, "Down, down, baby, down by the roller coaster." Emily watches them, but the way her fingers tap the table tells Joe her mind's on something else.

"What happens after Austin?" he asks.

"After what?" she says.

"Austin."

"We drive back to L.A."

"And after that?"

"We clean up our messes."

"Are we still gonna be friends?"

"I hope so," Emily says.

This isn't the answer Joe was expecting. He pulls down the hat she hates and tilts his head back to squint at her from under the brim.

"What happened to Nicaragua?" he says.

"Even if I don't go, you should," she says.

"I feel like drinking whiskey," he says.

Emily films the big rigs lit up like carnival rides that roar past them on their walk to the liquor store. The wind has returned, hot and pushy. Black clouds limned with moonglow roll in, blotting out the stars, and trash skitters down the road. A sheet of Tyvek that's been torn loose from the wall of a building under construction snaps like someone cracking a whip.

"Better batten down the hatches," says the old man who rings up Joe's fifth of whatever's cheapest. "We're getting some weather this evening."

"A tornado hit here, didn't it?" Joe says.

"In 1970," the old man says. "Killed twenty-six people and destroyed half the city."

"My grandpa told me about it," Joe says to Emily. "His cousin died in it."

"What?" Emily says.

"I just remembered."

"You should go see the memorial then, across Q there, next to Denny's," the old man says. He points out the store's window.

Joe and Emily stop at the memorial on their way back to the motel. A concrete plaza is imprinted with a map of the city, and two twenty-foot-high granite walls trace the paths of the pair of twisters that touched down on the night of May 11, 1970. The names of the victims and stories from survivors are etched into the granite. Emily searches for Joe's relative.

"What was his name?" she asks him.

"My grandpa's last name was Rains," he says. "Buck Rains. I think it was his cousin, his cousin's wife, and their kids who were killed, but all I really remember is they found their baby a mile from the house, wrapped in a sheet of tin."

Nobody named Rains is listed on the walls. Emily wants to film Joe repeating the story his grandfather told him, but he says no. He tells her about Matt back in L.A., how he recorded a lot of his stories and said he would do something with them.

"So what happened?" Emily says.

"Nothing," Joe says. "He's a fuckup."

They each take a belt of whiskey, toasting the town's dead. An eyeball-searing flash of lightning startles them, followed closely by a clap of thunder so loud it shakes Joe's bones. The one-two punch knocks him back to Nasiriyah for a second. Panic rockets like a piston from his gut to his throat, but he heads it off by trying to remember that thing where you can determine how far away a lightning strike is by counting the time between the flash and the sound of thunder. What is it? Two seconds is a mile? Three seconds? Ten?

Rain pours down, the drops hitting the ground so hard, a waist-high mist rises. Joe and Emily run all the way to the motel, but even so they're soaked when they get there. Emily, worried about tornadoes, turns on the TV to check for warnings.

They change out of their wet clothes and, after the downpour stops as suddenly as it began, sit on the walkway with the whiskey and a joint, counting together when lightning forks in the distance. One Mississippi. Two Mississippi. Emily Googled it: Five seconds between a flash and rumble means the strike was a mile away.

The construction workers are all in bed, their rooms dark.

"There's one of them lying awake, scared shitless by this storm," Emily says. "There's got to be."

July 20, 1:15 a.m.

If you use this one, change the guy's name. In fact, I'll
change it now — call him Bob.

It's only you and me here.

Yeah, but you're recording. I don't want to get sued.

That's blow talking.

Me and Bob used to clean pools together and go out
drinking afterward. One night he said he had a business proposition for me. This jack shack he went to in
East Hollywood was up for sale.

Jack shack?

A massage parlor where they give hand jobs.

You go to those?

Fuck no. I've never paid for sex in my life. Chicks who
do that shit hate the guys who pay them for it, and why
would I pay to fuck someone who hates me? Just listen.
The place was gonna cost twelve grand, and Bob was
figuring a couple thousand more for improvements.
His big thing was buying better towels, because the
ones the old owner made the girls use were like sandpaper. He thought if he bumped up to nice, soft towels,
it'd give the joint some class and lead to more repeat
business. His other thing was, he was dating one of the
girls who worked there, this Thai chick — all the girls
were Thai — and he was gonna make her the new
Mama-san. He figured she wouldn't rip him off because she was his girlfriend.

A real genius, huh?

Right. That's why I said "Thanks, but no thanks" when he asked me to kick in six grand and partner up with him—and I even had the money. "Be careful," I told him. "You don't know anything about this racket." But he was all, "Dude. It's a business like any other business." The way he saw it, he'd put in twelve thousand and some fluffy towels and kick back and watch the money roll in.

Don't break my heart.

Pull yourself a Kleenex, bro. The day after he took over, the cops showed up with their hands out. Okay, he thought, that's the cost of doing business. A little for them, a lot more for me. A few days later two Thai gangsters were at the door. They told him all the girls working there belonged to them, and they wanted their cut. Bob got on the phone to the cops he'd paid off and said, "I need your help," but they were like, "Sorry." Bob asked them what the fuck he was paying them for then, and they said, "To look the other way. Any problems you have are your own." Next up was the Armenian mob, who told him he had to pay a tax to operate a whorehouse in their territory. Bob sat down and thought things over. At that point any money he'd have made off the place would've gone to the cops, the pimps, and these Armenians. So what did he do? He said "Fuck all y'all," didn't pay anybody, and a week later the joint burned down.

Who torched it?

Take your pick. But, see, in the movie, you've gotta have Bob fight back, not run away to Seattle. You've gotta make him a badass.

It's a tragedy, really. He was a man with a dream.

He was a dipshit who thought he was smarter than he was. His dream should've been a week in Cabo. His dream should've been dental implants. If you get greedy like he did, you'll end up choking on your own tongue every time.

21: DIRTY SIXTH

THE NEXT DAY DAWNS STILL, CLEAR, AND HOT. BY EIGHT A.M. there aren't even any puddles left. Joe replaces the soggy cardboard in the truck's window, and he and Emily grab bagels and coffee from the motel's free breakfast and set out early, before another dust storm whips up. It'll be a six-hour drive to Austin.

Something's troubling Emily. She barely says a word and curls into a ball against her door as soon as they're in the truck. Joe doesn't bother asking what's wrong this time. He's come to the conclusion her mood swings don't have much to do with him and the best thing to do is ride them out.

After an hour on the road, she sits up and checks her phone.

"Did you let your ex know you're coming?" Joe asks her.

"I don't have a signal," she says.

"I mean before, earlier," Joe says.

She doesn't reply.

"Did you?" Joe says.

"What do you think?" she snaps. "Of course I did!"

Joe redirects the pulse of anger that tightens his jaw, sending it coursing down his arms and out through his fingertips. He flashes back to the prison self-help class where he learned the technique and the goofy fucker who explained it. Big teeth, smeared glasses—Tom, Tim. "Keep your mind on what's important," Tim would say. "Don't let a temper tantrum knock you off course."

What's important today is getting Emily to her daughter, so if she does something that bothers him, he'll ignore it. If she says something that stings, he'll bite his tongue. They're so close to Austin after having come all this way, it'd be a terrible failure to let rage get the best of him now.

The scenery on this leg of the trip consists of fields that go on forever and one tiny farm town after another, all identical. Every so often a few cows or a tractor provides some variety. Outside Santa Anna, a rickety yellow biplane swoops low to dust rows of cotton plants with something that settles like a thick fog. Emily rouses herself again to close every dashboard vent within reach. Joe's been seeing signs for a barbecue joint up ahead. He asks if she wants to stop for lunch and takes her shrug for a yes.

The place isn't much more than a shack with a crusty smoker out front and three picnic tables. Emily sits in the shade, sullen behind her sunglasses, while Joe orders. She only picks at her brisket when he delivers it.

"Everything's gonna be fine," he says. "Don't freak yourself out."

"I'm trying not to," she says.

He ordered her a beer, but she doesn't want that either, so he drinks it after finishing his own and walks out to the parking lot to smoke. Beyond a barbed-wire fence lies a fallow field. Joe steps behind a bush and pisses between the strands of the fence, aiming at an evil-looking weed. It puts him in mind of something he saw on TV about the ancient Romans, how they'd plow up their conquered enemies' fields and taint the soil with salt so nothing would grow there again. Emily's sitting with her head in her hands when he returns to the table. He pitches her brisket into a trash can swarming with yellowjackets.

As soon as they're back in the truck, Emily puts in her earbuds and slides over against the door again. Joe settles behind the wheel, ready for the final push. He comes up with various diversions to keep his mind from straying into dark places during the long, silent drive, like cataloging all the license plates from different states that he sees and dealing imaginary poker hands and running through betting strategies.

The country changes as they near Austin. They wind through rocky hills covered with mesquite, oak, and juniper trees. They skirt a lake, cross a river, and pass gated neighborhoods of big new houses with circular driveways and stone chimneys. At the city limits, not knowing if Emily's asleep or awake, Joe lays a hand on her shoulder. She sits up, takes off her sunglasses, and stares at him like he's a stranger.

"Where to?" he says.

"I want to stay somewhere nice," she says. "I'm tired of being scared."

"You were scared?" he says.

She gets on her phone and directs him to a Hilton. Austin surprises him after days of dirt, rock, and scrub. He wasn't expecting a city with freeways, with buses and new high-rises. They get caught in the afternoon rush hour and spend twenty minutes inching along in heavy traffic. The slowdown upsets Emily. She goes from near catatonic to bouncing in her seat.

Ignoring her agitation, Joe says, "Have you been here before?"

"A hundred years ago," she says. "For South by Southwest."

"What's that? A music thing?"

"Music, film, art. I was chasing this guy, a director, and I made a complete fucking fool of myself. Fortunately, I can't remember most of it."

"There's nothing wrong with forgetting," Joe says. "If a memory drags you down, let it go." More prison-shrink wisdom.

"I don't remember it because I was wasted the whole time," Emily says.

Joe changes the subject, says, "I've never stayed at a Hilton before."

"Yeah, because you never had a rich girlfriend before," Emily says.

"I may be poor," Joe says, "but I've got a big dick." He's hoping for a laugh but doesn't get one.

Emily's hands flutter around her face until she traps them between her legs. "I'm gonna peel my skin off if we don't get out of this traffic," she says.

The hotel is downtown in a tall building with two wings of rooms and a pool on the roof. Parking's forty dollars a day, so Joe can only imagine what Emily's paying for the room. He wanders around the lobby while she checks in. People are packed into the bar for happy hour, everyone wearing name tags. Joe asks the bartender how much a beer costs. He feels like he should conserve what cash he has left but a four-dollar Bud isn't going to break the bank.

Two women down the bar, a blonde with bright red lipstick

and elaborate eye makeup and a bruiser with a purple mullet, watch him order and pay, whispering to each other behind their hands. Joe turns to them and grimaces like he would to scare a kid. They laugh, and the bruiser asks if he's in a band.

"No," he says. "Are you?"

Kathy, the bruiser, and Amber are in from Chicago for an EMT conference at the convention center next door to the hotel. They're sales reps for a company that makes a new kind of heart monitor. Kathy asks Joe what brought him to town.

"I'm doing a good deed," he says.

The women are about to run off to catch a boat for a cruise on a nearby lake. Every night at sunset a million bats living under a bridge that spans the lake all fly out at once to hunt for insects. It's supposed to be quite a sight. After that the women are going to Sixth Street, where there are a bunch of restaurants and bars.

"You've never heard of it?" Amber says. "It's famous. Better than Bourbon Street."

"Sounds like the place to be," Joe says.

Kathy makes him put her number into his phone. "If you go over there, text us," she says. "We need a bodyguard."

A message from Emily pops up: *Where are you?*

"It's happy hour," he says when he rejoins her in the lobby. "Let's get happy."

"I'm going up to the room," she says.

"Can I come too?" he says, still joking around.

"Do what you want," she says.

He rolls with the punch. Can't hurt steel.

The room's on the tenth floor. There are two soft queen beds with white duvets, a big TV, and a couch in a sitting area with a floor-to-ceiling window looking out over the city. Joe replaces the drinks in the mini-fridge with the Bud left over from last night. He gets the whiskey out of his bag and rustles up glasses, real ones, not plastic. Emily says she doesn't want the snort he pours her, but he insists.

"We made it," he says. "Let's celebrate."

Emily downs the whiskey and says, "I talked to my ex."

"So, what's the plan?" Joe asks her.

"I can see Phoebe tomorrow morning."

"That's great."

Emily smiles for the first time today. It's quick, and it's sad, but it's a smile. Joe's sitting on the arm of the couch. She walks over and stands between his legs. "We had a little fun, didn't we?" she says.

"Come on," Joe says. "I finally saw the Grand Canyon, which you're supposed to see when you're like five. I saw fucking Lubbock, Texas."

Emily's smile is still there, but there's nothing behind it. An uneasiness comes over Joe, rank and sticky like flop sweat, creeping dread out of nowhere.

"Pour me another drink," Emily says.

Joe walks to the dresser where the bottle sits, but more whiskey isn't going to help him shake his black thoughts. He needs room to outrun them.

"Hey," he says to Emily. "Do you know about this bridge with the bats?"

The Congress Avenue Bridge turns out to be a short walk from the hotel. It's easy to find because everyone on the street, laughing people swigging beer and margaritas from plastic cups, is headed there. The evening's hot and humid, but a cool breeze takes the edge off Joe's jimjams. *We'll get through this okay,* he thinks. *Please let us get through this okay.*

The deal is, you stand on the bridge to watch the bats fly out from underneath it, but the bridge's walkways are already packed with spectators. Some dude tells Joe there's a better view from a bike path that runs along the shore of the lake below. It's crowded there too, but Joe squeezes himself and Emily into a spot on the rail.

The sun's sinking fast, and kayakers and tourist boats on the lake jockey for position near the bridge. On the bike path, a loudmouth decked out in sports swag for a team Joe doesn't recognize uses a selfie stick to take a picture of himself and his wife; two teenagers sit cross-legged on the ground, playing cards; and a woman changes her baby's diaper on a bench. Joe smells the shit from the diaper, and the buzzing of cicadas is like a rasp working on his brain. There are too many people and too much going on. He needs to find someplace less frantic where he can pull himself together, but he doesn't want to let on to Emily that he's not a hundred percent on a night when she's having trouble of her own.

Right before sunset, the crowd murmurs and points their phones at a few bats that trickle out from under the bridge. Another twenty or so emerge, and anticipation builds for the coming flood, hundreds of thousands of the little creatures billowing into a manic black cloud and swirling higher and higher before flapping off into the new-fallen night. But, no, that's it. No more bats appear.

The crowd turns surly when it realizes the show is already over.

"What a rip!" a woman with a kid on her shoulders shouts.

"Maybe it's the weather," Joe says to Emily.

"Let's go," Emily says. "I'm hungry."

They walk up the stairs to the street. Emily lights a joint and hits it out in the open.

"Share that shit," a passing asshole shouts.

"You want my herpes too?" Emily shouts back, then coughs and cackles at her own quip.

They proceed to Sixth Street, which turns out to be exactly what Joe expected: five blocks of neon, loud music, and tourist bars pushing two-for-one drink specials. It being Sunday, most of the bars are dead, and the atmosphere is that of a deserted carnival, with as many homeless staggering down the sidewalk as college students and conventioneers.

Emily's determined to find the restaurant where she had the greatest queso ever last time she was here. She starts her search on the south side of the street, poking her head into every eatery she and Joe come to, but none matches her memory. She insists on checking the other side of the street too, and pitches a fit when they get back to where they began and she still hasn't located the place.

Joe's had enough. He steers her into the first restaurant they come to, a hip two-story Tex-Mex joint with neon cacti, a mariachi band, and mango habanero margaritas. They have their choice of tables. Emily picks one on the second-floor terrace, overlooking the street, and tries to order a margarita and an extra shot of tequila from the hostess, who says she'll send a waitress over. Joe decides he better stick to beer.

When the food arrives, Emily spits the queso she ordered into her napkin and pushes aside her chile relleno after one bite.

"This is shit," she says.

"Eat it anyway," Joe says. "You need to get something in your stomach."

"I need another drink."

"No, you don't. You're seeing Phoebe tomorrow. That'll be stressful enough without being hungover."

"I'll be in fine shape," Emily says. "Shipshape, shit-shape, shipshape."

"Seriously," Joe says.

"Seriously?" Emily says, a razor glint in her eye. She picks up her empty shot glass and tosses it over the rail of the terrace.

"Get up," Joe says, standing himself. "We're leaving."

"I'm not going anywhere," Emily says.

"You're on your own then," Joe says. "I'm not waiting around for the cops to come."

"What are you afraid of, jailbird?"

Feeling like he's about to explode, Joe turns without another word and walks down the stairs. He's half a block away from the restaurant before his brain catches up to his body. As much as he'd like to go back to the hotel, get in the truck, and drive away, he can't leave Emily out here by herself, where she's likely to end up in the kind of trouble that'll keep her from seeing her daughter tomorrow. Groaning with the effort, he forces himself to return to the restaurant.

Emily's already out on the sidewalk when he gets there. She bursts into tears when she sees him. He puts his arms around her, and she clings to him like everything in the world's trying to pull her away.

"I'm sorry," she sobs.

"We're going back to the hotel and get a good night's sleep," he says. "You'll be fine in the morning."

"What the fuck is fine?" she says.

Joe can't answer that, but one thing he does know is that when you most want to stop is when you've got to keep moving, so that's what they do. It feels like they're walking into the wind all the way back to the hotel, like there's mud sucking at their shoes, but they make it.

July 15, 1:37 a.m.

Do you believe in God?

I don't even think about shit like that.

You don't wonder what's gonna happen to you when you
 die?

I could give a fuck.

Heaven and hell?

If there's a hell, everyone I've ever met is going there. If
 there's a heaven, it's only for dogs.

22: THE DARK END
OF THE STREET

THEY GO STRAIGHT TO BED. EMILY SLEEPS FOR A WHILE, BUT then she's awake, toying with her phone or reading her book every time Joe comes to during the night. He asks once if she's okay and lets her be after that, wary of upsetting her.

When he opens his eyes at eight a.m., she's sitting on the second bed fully dressed and staring out the window.

"What time do you see Phoebe?" he asks her.

"Later," she replies. "I'm going for a walk now."

He sees that her bag is packed. This sets off all kinds of alarms. "I'll go with you," he says.

"No," she says.

She gets up, takes the handle of her bag, and starts for the door.

"Where are you going?" Joe says, scrambling out of bed. She doesn't answer. Joe puts his hand on the door, not letting her open it. "Wait a second," he says. "Tell me what's happening."

"Get out of my way," Emily says. She grabs his wrist and digs in with her fingernails.

He pulls away and hurries to dress as she fumbles with the lock. She's dragging her bag down the hall by the time he gets his shoes on. He jogs to close the distance between them and stands behind her while she frantically punches the elevator call button.

"Look at me," he says.

She acts like he's not there.

"If you don't want to be around me, stay here and I'll split," he says. "You don't have to go."

The elevator doors open. Two men in suits step back to let Emily and Joe in. Emily pushes the button for the lobby though it's already lit, and the doors close.

"Let's have coffee and talk about this," Joe says in a loud whisper.

When the elevator doors open again, Emily rushes out.

"Excuse me," one of the suit guys calls after her, eyeing Joe. "Is everything okay?"

"Mind your own fucking business," Joe snarls before racing after Emily as she charges across the lobby.

Outside, she hurries down the sidewalk like she knows where she's going. Joe follows a few yards behind her. He notices she's barefoot.

"At least stop and put on some shoes," he says. "You look like a crazy person."

"Leave me alone!" she screams.

A block from the hotel the sidewalk ends and the street narrows. Railroad tracks run beside the asphalt. Joe and Emily detour around a construction site and walk under a freeway. It feels like they're already on the edge of the city. A Target store and new condos are going up to their left, but to the right, across the tracks, it's all junkyards, warehouses, and empty lots. Joe catches up to Emily and grabs her arm.

"Look at me, that's all I'm asking," he says.

"Let go of me and back off, and I will," she says.

He retreats five paces with his hands in the air. She turns to face him.

"You have to let me go," she says.

"Why?" he says.

"This was a mistake."

"What was?"

"This trip, you, everything."

Joe forces a smile. "What are you talking about?" he says. "You're gonna see Phoebe."

Emily's face ripples like a puddle scoured by a cold wind. "There is no Phoebe," she says.

Joe ponders what this might mean. Before he can ask, Emily speaks again.

"There's no ex-husband, either," she says. "All of that was lies."

"So what the fuck are we doing here?" Joe says.

"I don't know," Emily says. "I wanted to get away from my sister? I wanted to take a trip? I wanted to be with you?"

"Did you? Want to be with me?"

"I said I don't know."

A dog barks somewhere in the distance. Two guys in yellow reflective vests and hardhats play-wrestle on the loading dock of the Target. The morning's getting hotter by the second, and sweat skitters down Joe's back as he tries to decide what else to say. All he comes up with is "So can we go back to L.A. now?" Emily doesn't answer. A commuter train approaches on the tracks. The wrestlers stop to watch it. Joe watches it too. One of the cars screeches as it passes over a torqued rail, making him wince.

"Don't hate me," Emily says, and runs off without her bag.

It takes Joe a second to wrap his head around where she's headed. When he figures it out, he sprints after her. The tracks are at ground level, not elevated on a bed of crushed rock. Emily races along beside them toward the train. Joe gains on her but knows he won't catch up in time.

"Stop!" he yells.

The train keeps on coming, looming larger and larger, as unstoppable as a murderer's bullet. Joe's twelve feet behind Emily when she steps in front of it. He closes his eyes, claps his hands over his ears, and turns away, screaming wordlessly over the blare of the train's horn and the squeal of its brakes. He's still screaming when everything quiets down. He refills his lungs and opens his eyes to see the wrestlers gaping, open-mouthed.

"Holy shit!" one of them yells. "Holy shit!"

Joe turns slowly, a hand raised to block his view in case what's revealed is too awful. He's standing next to the third car in the train. It took that long to stop. He lowers his gaze to the rails, expecting blood, expecting gore, but there's nothing. He stumbles toward the front of the train, thinking any second he'll see her body. When he reaches the lead car, he looks under it.

"You know there's cameras on here," the driver, a Latina, shouts down from the window of her compartment. "It's all on the computer, her fucking around like that. If any passengers are hurt, she's responsible."

"Where'd she go?" Joe says.

"She crossed in front of me and ran off that way," the driver says, gesturing vaguely.

Still having trouble squaring what happened with what he'd been expecting, Joe crosses the tracks himself and scans the area. He calls Emily's name while jogging toward a recycling center in a fenced-in lot on a road that runs parallel to the tracks. A security guard stands behind an eight-foot gate.

"Did you see a woman come by?" Joe asks him.

"When?" the guard says.

"A few seconds ago. Curly hair, barefoot."

"I just got back from the can."

"Can I come in and look for her?"

"You have to have an appointment."

The train's moving again, continuing on its way. Joe keeps walking and yelling for Emily. He comes to a plot of vacant land overgrown with head-high brush. A narrow, trampled trail leads into the thicket. He takes it.

The trail ends in a clearing containing a tent, a decrepit couch, and a two-burner propane stove. Rocks arranged in a circle form a fire pit, and damp clothing hangs from a line strung between the trunks of two trees. A little bald guy with a bushy beard and wild eyes pops up. He brandishes a screwdriver like a knife.

"Halt!" he yelps.

"Did a woman come through here?" Joe asks him.

"There's no women here, man. No women allowed."

Joe retraces his steps along the trail. When he reaches the road, he walks on, shouting for Emily. He checks behind a dumpster and under a boarded-up house, anywhere she might be hiding. He hits a cross street, looks up and down it, hits another, and realizes that if she really wanted to get away, she's long gone by now.

The sun's doing a number on him. He's dizzy, and his shirt is soaked with sweat. He ducks into a corner market for a bottle of water and asks the woman at the register if she's seen Emily. She hasn't. Returning to where Emily crossed the tracks, he retrieves her bag and starts walking back to the hotel on the chance she went there.

He pulls the bag behind him. The plastic wheels click-clack over the cracks in the sidewalk. Normal life goes on. People hurry to their jobs, people wait in line to order coffee. A van stops at the curb, and the driver hops out to deliver a package. A gardener waters one of the hotel's flower beds. Joe feels far away from it all, like it's something he's watching on TV.

He opens the door to the room hopeful, but Emily's not there. He could alert the police, but that might lead to trouble for both of them. A call to Emily's phone goes to voice mail. "Please let me know you're okay," he says, and texts the same thing. He begins to think more clearly as he cools down. He calls the front desk and asks how long the room was booked for. One more night. That's good. That's great. Emily has plenty of time to make her way back.

There's a room-service menu on the table in front of the couch. He's never ordered room service before, but charging a meal now will help him conserve his cash. The woman on the phone says his bacon, eggs, and coffee will be up in half an hour.

The breakfast would be a treat if Emily were here, but things being the way they are, the food's merely fuel. He shoves as much of it into himself as he can, almost choking on the toast. The cigarette he smokes in front of the hotel afterward is rough too. Every so often he'll have one he's sure is the one that's going to flip the cancer switch. This is one of those.

He spends the day watching TV and checking his phone every five minutes. He texts Emily three more times but gets no response, and his calls to her continue to be routed to voice mail, where they're answered by the same greeting she's had since they met: "This is Emily, and whatever I'm doing now isn't as important as talking to you, so leave a message, and I'll get back to you." The first time he begs her again to get in touch with him. After that he hangs up when the recording begins.

Every hour that passes that he doesn't hear from her ratchets up his anxiety. A knock at the door around eleven has him falling all over himself to answer, startling a housekeeper, who asks if he wants her to make the bed. He orders again from room service about three, a bacon cheeseburger. About six he drinks two of his beers from the mini-fridge and kills the bottle of whiskey he bought in Lubbock.

The sun's setting when he goes downstairs for a smoke. People are on the move, headed to the bridge to see the bats or to Sixth Street for dinner. Watching them pass by, he comes up with a plan: He'll retrace his and Emily's steps from last night on the chance she returns to somewhere they were yesterday. It's a long shot, but anything'll be better than sitting around waiting. He leaves a note on the bed in case she shows up while he's gone.

Another crowd has gathered to see the bats, and the same tourist boats are parked under the bridge. Joe walks up and down the bank where he and Emily stood last night, scanning the spectators that fill the bike path and the grassy hill beside it. The first few bats take wing as he's crossing the bridge. He has to step off the sidewalk and into traffic to get around the people lined up there. Emily's not among them, and she's not in the park on the other side of the lake where more people have congregated. The swarm fails to appear again this evening, and disappointment's spreading through the crowd when Joe recrosses the bridge on his way to Sixth Street.

He starts at the west end of the strip of bars and restaurants. At the first club he comes to, the doorman informs him there's a ten-dollar cover.

"I'll only be a second," Joe says. "I'm looking for a missing woman."

"Sorry, boss, ten bucks," the doorman says.

Joe opens his wallet, takes out the photo-booth photo of Emily from the Short Stop.

"Here she is," he says to the doorman. "Have you seen her?"

The doorman barely glances at the picture. "Nope," he says. "You coming in? I got people behind you."

A white blues band is playing in the next bar. The place is empty, but Joe shows one of the bartenders the photo. The girl's wearing earplugs and has a hard time hearing his questions. She hasn't seen Emily either.

After stopping into three more joints, Joe realizes he's spinning his wheels. He turns onto the first quiet street he comes to and goes into the first quiet bar, a worn-out shotgun dive, stick on the right, booths on the left. Music's playing, Johnny Cash, but thankfully down low on an antique jukebox. Nobody's there but an old lady bartender and two old men. It's eight bucks for a beer and a shot. Joe downs his first round with the bartender still standing in front of him and orders another.

"You ain't gonna give me trouble, are you?" the bartender asks him.

"Ma'am, I'm a professional," he replies. "You won't even know I'm here."

One of the old men is very drunk. He doubles over and presses his forehead to the bar. Joe at first thinks he's laughing, but he's not, he's crying.

"I'm sorry," he calls to Joe when the worst has passed. "My brother died today."

I can't handle this, Joe thinks, but he doesn't get up and go. He stays for hours and blows through fifty bucks listening to Willie Nelson, George Jones, and the Flying Burrito Brothers sing all the dead brother's favorite songs. The sidewalk pitches like the deck of a ship in a storm during his stumble back to the hotel. He zigzags his way along, teetering once or twice on the curb and talking nonsense to the moon. He knows Emily won't be in the room but is disappointed all the same when she isn't. Thankfully, it doesn't last long. He's asleep within ten minutes, passes out watching poker on TV.

August 5, 11:13 p.m.

Why you playing this?

It's *Dark Side of the Moon*. A classic. What's your problem?

It was my dad's favorite album. I remember me and him driving down Van Nuys in his truck and him blasting it. It used to scare the shit out of me, how it starts off, that heartbeat and laughing. I was like five and like, "What the fuck is this?" He'd sing along, [singing himself] "Money, it's a gas," which now I'd ask him, "How the fuck do you know? You never had any." He sold blood to bet on horses. He traded our vacuum cleaner for coke and blamed my mom when she found out. "You wouldn't give me fifty bucks. What was I supposed to do?"

Sounds like a wild man.

Sounds like a fucking psycho. He got in fights every time he stepped out of the house, came to blows over a parking spot at the grocery store, knocked a dude out because he cut in line at IHOP.

What was his problem?

My mom says he blamed everything on his childhood. His mother ran off, and him and his brother were raised by their grandma. He never met his dad but claimed he was some rich dude and was always thinking he would show up someday and lay a load of money on him. My mom says all that was bullshit though.

Why'd she marry him?

Why do you think?

Widdle Joe came along?

I don't care if she was sixteen, I don't care if her mom
pushed her into it, she should've had an abortion. It
was a crime to bring a child into a situation like that.

We've all made bad decisions.

Like murdering your brother while your six-year-old son
is waiting in the car?

Wait, what?

I already told you this a week ago. My dad? Check your
recordings.

I don't think so. I'd remember.

Come on, dude, how me and him went over to his brother's, and he told me to stay in the car while he went
inside? The ice cream truck song?

I'm telling you—

While I was sitting there an ice cream truck drove by
playing that song [hums "Turkey in the Straw"], and
every time I hear it now, I get chills. I didn't hear him
shoot, but I knew something was wrong because he
was all hyped up when he came back out. He'd promised to take me to In-N-Out, and that's what we did,
went and got burgers. On the way there a cop got
behind us, and my dad told me if we got pulled over to
lay on the floor of the car and not get up.

Dude was gonna shoot it out?

Luckily, it was a false alarm. He dropped me off at home
and took off, and I never saw him again. They arrested
him in Vegas a week later. Him and his brother had
argued about some money somebody owed someone,
and he shot him in the head.

You didn't visit him? In prison?

Are you kidding? I was scared shitless of him after that,
and my mom cut him off completely. Turned out she

already had a boyfriend. They got married six months after he was arrested.

Wow.

He was dead by then anyway, got stabbed before he was even sentenced. God needed another angel, I guess. [He laughs.] Seriously, though, he was doomed from the start. It didn't matter about his childhood. He was what he was from the second he clawed his way out of his mom.

An outlaw.

Fuck that. He didn't *choose* to break the law or go against society's rules. He didn't even *know* the rules. If he wanted something, he took it. If someone pissed him off, he went after them. He was a fucking jackal, and jackals don't last long. They don't hide what they are because they can't. They steal or rape or kill until they get put down.

23: GOD, GUNS, AND GUTS

When Emily hasn't shown up by the next morning, Joe tries to contact her sister in L.A. It's a bust. He knows what street she lives on, North Catalina, and Emily's last name, Mercer, but an internet search turns up nothing. He can't think of anything else to do after this but go back to L.A. He's got less than a hundred bucks in cash left and only three hundred dollars in his account, but that should be enough for food and gas. He packs up—takes Emily's suitcase too—and leaves after another room-service breakfast. It's a straight shot up the 10. Twenty hours, 1,300 miles. With no fucking around, he can do it in two long, long days.

Texas turns drier and dustier the farther west he drives. He goes an hour without seeing a real tree. Plenty of roadkill though. Deer, jackrabbits, a gory mess that was either a coyote or a dog, buzzards squabbling over the pieces. He leaves the radio off. The tires on the road, the hum of the engine, and a whistle coming from a gap in the tape holding the broken-window cardboard in place are music enough.

Three hours in he stops at a gas station to fill the truck and buy beef jerky and a six-pack of tall Bud Lights. He shoots one of the beers crouched beside the station's dumpster. The wind's blowing so hard, it takes four tries to light a cigarette. A horned toad, doing nervous push-ups, watches him smoke.

"Don't worry, dude," he says. "I'm not after your flies."

A strip of jerky and another beer stave off his hunger during the next leg of the drive. He eats and swigs on straight sections of the highway, steering with his knees. The only slowdown is an overturned big rig on the shoulder near Van Horn. The right lane's closed, and orange cones funnel traffic. A bored highway patrolman waves the looky-loos along. The doors to the truck's trailer popped open, and its load of breakfast cereal spilled out. The asphalt around the wreck is speckled with a colorful confetti of pulverized Apple Jacks, Froot Loops, and Frosted Flakes.

After eight hours, he's still in Texas. He pulls into another gas station to take a piss and stumbles and almost falls getting out of the truck. His feet are numb, and he can't straighten his back. He stretches, reaching as high as he can, then pulls each knee in toward his chest. This loosens things up enough that he can hobble through the station's store to the restroom. Afterward, he tops off the tank. It'll be dark in a couple hours, and he doesn't want to run out of gas at night in the middle of nowhere.

It's six p.m. when he sets out again. The sun, dropping quickly, shines into his eyes even with the visor down. Near El Paso the freeway runs along the border. On the Mexican side street after street of cinderblock and stucco boxes stretch as far south as he can see, while the hills in the U.S. are covered with Spanish-style tract homes aglow in a fiery dusk. In Ciudad Juarez, three kids ride bikes past a baby-blue body shop. In El Paso, tennis players volley on courts scalded by bright white lights. Joe's cheered by the glimpses of civilization, but the road soon shoots off again into barrenness.

He chases the setting sun into New Mexico, where it finally outruns him and sinks below the horizon, leaving a persistent orange glow in its wake that keeps the stars at bay. His legs ache like they did when growing pains tortured him as a boy. He hits Deming as night finally falls. He's starting to see things—animals darting across the road, cars where there aren't any, hitchhikers out of the corner of his eye. Better to stop here than keep going until he nods out behind the wheel.

A Walmart Supercenter sits right off the freeway. He's heard travelers can park for free there overnight. He spots some RVs at the edge of the store's lot and drives toward them. An old man in a Make America Great Again hat is sitting in a camp chair outside a beat-up Winnebago, a grizzled Chihuahua trembling in his lap. The dog croaks at Joe as he gets out of the F-150.

"Sugar Bear," the old man scolds.

"Will anybody hassle me if I sleep in my truck here tonight?" Joe asks him.

"Not if you behave yourself," the old man says. "And if you don't, I'll chase you off myself."

Joe sticks out his hand. "I'm Joe."

"Warren," the old man says, leaning forward to shake. "You a veteran?"

"I am," Joe says.

"Thank you for your service."

Joe gets his legs working again walking across the lot to the store's entrance. The aisles are deserted, but it feels to Joe like they were bustling only seconds ago and everyone disappeared as soon as he came inside. His footsteps ring out as he proceeds to the grocery section. He grabs a sub wrapped in plastic and a bag of Doritos. He buys more beer, too.

The girl who rings him up is slim and pretty but has a droopy eyelid. He met a stripper once who had the same thing. He wanted to ask her if the eye affected her tips one way or the other but realized right before he did that it was a fucked-up question.

He eats sitting on the tailgate of the truck, tracking the moths dive-bombing the parking lot's lights. Someone's watching TV in one of the RVs, *American Ninja Warrior*. Joe can hear the announcers' voices and see the screen flashing behind a curtain. He hides his beer when a security guard approaches in a golf cart. The guard waves but doesn't stop.

Warren's still outside. Joe walks over and offers him a beer.

"I don't drink no more," Warren says.

"Good," Joe says. "More for me."

"Where you headed?"

"California. L.A."

"What the hell for?"

Joe shrugs. "It's home. It's where I live."

"What kind of work you do?"

"Construction, painting, bartending."

"I drove a truck. Now I play poker. I'm on my way to Laughlin for a tournament."

"You do okay?"

"I'd tell you yes," Warren says, "but one look at this piece of shit"—he jerks his thumb at the Winnebago—"and you'd know I was lying."

The dog in his lap lifts its ears and growls.

"What is it, girl?" Warren says. He squints into the surrounding darkness. "Two meth heads came around panhandling earlier," he says to Joe, opening his windbreaker to show a pistol tucked into his jeans. "This here's shorthand for 'I told you no once before. Now move the fuck along.'"

The dog loses interest in whoever or whatever roused it and again rests its head on Warren's thigh, its paws crossed like a pair of little hands.

"Where you coming from?" Warren asks Joe.

"Austin," Joe tells him.

"What were you doing there?"

"Good question."

"So it had something to do with a woman."

"It did," Joe says, "but I don't know what."

"Oh, come on," Warren says. "Don't play dumb with yourself."

Joe finishes his beer and walks back to the F-150. He climbs into the back seat and settles in. He's restless, though, can't get to sleep, and when he does, he dreams he's still driving.

About three he gets up and pisses as quietly as he can into a planter next to the truck. He leans against the hood and smokes a cigarette while looking up at the mess of stars filling the sky and wishes Emily was there to look at them with him. "Doesn't the freeway sound just like a river?" he'd say to her. Then he'd make a joke about whoever it is that's snoring in one of the RVs, call him Foghorn Leghorn.

Rousted by the rising sun, he washes up in the Walmart's bathroom, buys a Danish and a cup of coffee, and is on his way before the parking-lot ravens finish their morning shouting match. Arizona's a bright, dry blur. He gets more gas and coffee in Tucson and takes a longer break in Quartzsite, where he drinks a tall can of sweet tea, wolfs down two gas station hot dogs, and takes a stroll around town to loosen the knots in his back.

It's hotter than hell at three p.m., and the air is so still, the American flags that line the town's main street hang limply on their poles. Joe ducks into a shop that sells rocks and gems and bumper stickers touting God and guns. The desert rat behind the counter watches him like a hawk as he browses the bins of Apache tears, lepidolite, and carborundum. Wandering the aisles of a cluttered used bookstore, he thinks about buying a copy of *Anna Karenina* but can't puzzle out how the place is organized and doesn't want to ask the woman running the store where the book might be.

Before hitting the road again, he calls Mollin and asks if he can stay the night at his place. "Just you?" Mollin says.

"Just me," he replies.

"No problem."

The speedometer keeps creeping up to ninety on the last leg of the drive, as if the truck's rolling downhill. Joe does fine until he passes the wind turbines outside Palm Springs. That's where how hard he's been pushing finally catches up to him. During his final two hours behind the wheel, if he's not fighting to keep his eyes open, he's dealing with bouts of claustrophobia that have him writhing in his seat and gulping for air. He comes close to pulling over but pops a warm beer instead. *Just get to Fontana,* he tells himself, then, *Just get to Pomona,* then, *Just get to East L.A.*

He's flooded with relief when the downtown skyline finally comes into view, the familiar vista encompassing Griffith Park, the Hollywood Hills, and the flat grid of streets that sprawls all the way to the ocean. It's seven thirty. This time last night he was a grain of sand in a vast desert, a man who would've been lost without a dot on a map to show him where he was. But now he's home, where he knows all the streets and all the shortcuts, the places you go and those you don't, and the particular hue of the August evening sky. Now everything's going to be fine.

He drives straight to Emily's sister's house. There are lights on inside, and the Mini Emily drove is in the driveway, along with the sister's Discovery. He's weighed down by dread as he hauls Emily's suitcase up the stairs to the front door and worries there's beer on his breath. A few seconds after he rings the doorbell, the sister's voice comes out of it.

"Yes?"

"Hey," he says. "It's me. Joe. Emily's friend?"

"I know," the sister says. "I can see you."

"Do you know where Emily is?"

"Hold on."

Joe works himself up even more wondering what's coming next. His heart's pounding when the sister opens the door. She's wearing sweatpants and a T-shirt. Her hair is piled in a bun on top of her head.

"So you drove her to Austin?" she says.

"She told me she had a kid there, a daughter she wanted to see," Joe says.

"And you believed her?"

"Why wouldn't I?"

"Yeah, yeah," the sister says. She closes her eyes and pinches the bridge of her nose. Joe's seen Emily do the same thing.

"She freaked out when we got there and ran off," he says. "I waited and waited for her to come back, then drove here as fast as I could."

"Well, you can relax," the sister says. "She got back two nights ago."

"What happened?"

"She called after she left you, and I talked her into flying home and convinced her to go to a facility."

"So she's okay?"

"She's safe, and she's getting the help she needs."

Joe exhales loudly and shakes his head. "I've been so fucking worried," he says.

"I tried to warn you."

"Is there any way I can call her?"

"No."

"What do you mean?"

"I mean that's not going to happen, you calling or visiting or anything like that."

"Why not?" Joe says.

The sister makes a face like he's an idiot and says, "Dude! She's sick. She's not equipped to have a romantic relationship with you or anybody else."

"But I'm her friend."

"Well, I'm her sister, and I know more about what's good for her and what's not than you do."

"Will you at least give her a message?" Joe says.

"No," the sister says. "No messages, no calls, no nothing. It's over between you two, got it?"

Joe turns and goes, leaving the suitcase on the porch. He's humiliated, but relieved at the same time to know that Emily's alive. If he'd found out she'd gone through with it, had killed herself, it might have done *him* in. Lack of sleep and long hours behind the wheel have made him fragile. Traffic is insane on Los Feliz headed toward the 5. The rhythmic booming emanating from a little Toyota with a big subwoofer sets his teeth on edge, and missing a green light nearly breaks his heart.

★ ★ ★

Mollin has all kinds of questions, but Joe blows him off. They order a pizza and watch an old *Dateline*. Joe passes out before the killer's revealed.

Later that night he wakes in the bunk bed in the kids' room and has trouble getting back to sleep. He pulls up photos of the trip on his phone. There's one of Emily he really likes, where she's raising a hand to shield herself from the sun, a sweet grin on her face. He texts it to her with a message saying he talked to her sister and knows what happened. He says he's not mad at her and would love to hear from her when she's up to it. He wakes again later and thinks he's holding her in his arms, but it's only a pillow.

July 15, 2:01 a.m.

How old are you again?

Twenty-seven.

Well, let me tell you something: It goes very fucking fast from here on out. I can't believe I'm forty already and probably halfway through my life.

That's optimistic, hard as you party.

Yeah, fuck you. When I was younger, it was like I had all the time in the world. If I wasted a day here, a week there, it was no big deal. Now I'm on a runaway train. I'm still wasting time, but, man, I know it now and get so pissed at myself. Like, *You fucking idiot.*

What didn't you do that you wish you had?

I'm not talking about that. What bugs me is all the things I'm not gonna get to do because I'm gonna run out of time.

Like what?

Like I wanted to learn Spanish. But now it's too late. And kung fu. I should've started that as a kid. And magic.

Magic?

Coin tricks and shit. There's all this stuff I might've been great at. Who knows?

24: LIKE A HURRICANE

THE NEXT MORNING JOE GETS A CALL FROM ORI, A CONTRACtor he's worked for in the past. Ori's regular painter quit on him, and he asks if Joe can put together a crew by tomorrow to paint the interior of a house he's flipping in Sherman Oaks, a cash job, under the table. Joe drives out to look at the place and gives a low enough quote that he knows Ori will jump at it.

He hires two brothers from Michoacán to help him. They're better painters than he is and have all the gear he doesn't. The three of them bust their asses and finish the job in four days instead of the five Joe estimated. After paying for materials and settling with Max and Juanito, Joe has two grand left over and a promise from Ori of more work.

He calls Grady about replacing the window on the F-150. Grady says he'll do it for fifty bucks if Joe tracks down the glass. Joe finds a place in Reseda that has it for seventy dollars, and it takes Grady all of fifteen minutes to drop the new window in. A buddy of his is selling a twenty-year-old Civic for cheap. Joe calls the guy and talks him into letting him put five hundred dollars down and paying the rest in two weeks.

He spends the next morning washing and detailing the F-150, then calls Keith's wife. He tells her about Keith asking him to pick up the truck at Applebee's but leaves out the dope and the gun. He apologizes for holding on to the vehicle for so long, explaining that he freaked out after Keith died and got paranoid about cops.

"I'm an ex-con," he says, "so that's where my mind goes."

Keith's wife's as cold as ice, but she assures him the police won't be involved. Mollin agrees to follow him out to Norco, where the wife lives, if Joe will buy him a meal at the Old Spaghetti Factory in Duarte on their way back.

Keith's house is in a new development spread over the top of a rocky ridge with a view of the 15 freeway. Joe can't recall if he's met the wife before. She doesn't look familiar when she answers the door. He apologizes again for keeping the truck and says he's sorry about what happened to Keith.

"He was a good guy," he says.

"So I hear," the wife replies.

She walks out to the F-150 and circles it like she's looking for damage, even opening the door and peering inside the cab.

"I filled it up and washed it," Joe says.

"Thanks," she says.

The Duarte Spaghetti Factory is in an old schoolhouse. Mollin's a big fan of the chain. He's been to the ones in Salt Lake City, in Phoenix, in San Diego. He always orders the same thing, the Manager's Special with meat sauce and mizithra cheese. He and his sons used to come out here once a month, but now the boys are too busy. He doesn't make the trip by himself because he's uncomfortable eating in restaurants alone.

"I always imagine people looking at me and thinking, 'What's up with that pathetic piece of shit?'" he says.

"Is that what you think when you see someone eating by himself?" Joe asks him.

"Sometimes," he says.

"You're forty-two years old," Joe says. "What the fuck do you care what anyone thinks about you?"

Mollin asks again about Austin. It was a good trip, Joe tells him. Vegas, the Grand Canyon, Sixth Street.

"So the honeymoon went okay," Mollin says.

"The honeymoon went fine," Joe says.

"And your girl found somewhere to stay?"

"She's all squared away."

Joe gets Mollin talking about the restaurant again. The one in Fullerton's in an old train station. The one in Riverside was once a packing shed.

"I used to go to the Hollywood one with my mom," Joe says.

"That was my favorite," Mollin says. "I was so bummed when it closed. There's condos there now."

Joe starts looking for work, texting everyone he knows and hitting a couple bars a day to see if they're hiring. He confines his search to the Valley, because if he's at a joint over the hill, who's to say Danny Bones won't come strolling in some night? When Mollin gets home from Subway, the two of them lift weights, watch TV, and play video games, with Joe keeping it to one or two beers most evenings.

One of the bars he stops into is the Scoreboard, the sports bar that used to be McRed's, where he worked years ago. The manager calls two days later and asks if he's available to fill in for a bartender who's sick. Joe shows up and kills it, stepping in like he's been working there for years. He picks up another shift a few nights later, and the next week the manager offers him a full-time position.

He works Tuesday through Friday nights and opens Sundays at eleven a.m. The place serves food, and he's comped one meal per shift. The manager, Antoine, doesn't let the staff drink on duty, and Joe's fine with that. The rule keeps him in good enough shape that he's able to squeeze in painting gigs. Taking them means waking up at six a.m. after getting to bed at three and then grabbing another couple hours of sleep before reporting to the bar, but he's in no position to turn down work.

His cash reserve grows quickly, even after he gives Mollin a little something for letting him bunk at the house. He pays off the Civic, sells it to the barback at the Scoreboard, and buys a truck, a 2008 Ranger, for his painting jobs. He moves out of Mollin's house and into a single in Van Nuys, closer to the bar. The building's an ugly seventies cracker box, but the apartments have been refurbished, and there's parking. The other tenants are mostly Mexican families. Joe slips the old one-armed cholo who acts as the building's unofficial security guard a twelve-pack of Tecate every week in exchange for keeping an eye on his place when he's away, so nobody steals the TV and microwave he springs for.

And he gets laid. It's nothing he works on, just something that happens. Lola, a single mom from Honduras, is the designated driver for a bachelorette party at the bar one night. Joe gets to talking to her and mentions his new apartment. He's been sleeping on the floor because he's reluctant to buy furniture after losing more couches than he can count due to being evicted from places or having to move out in a hurry. Lola offers to help him decorate. She picks out a sofa bed and coffee table at Ikea, and sheets, towels, and dishes at Target. Then they go back to the apartment, get stoned, and break in the bed. The sex isn't great, but it's good enough for his first time since Emily. He worries Lola will want something serious afterward, but three days later she texts she's getting back with her daughter's father.

The days fall like dominos, and before he knows it, it's the Sunday before Christmas. He wakes up with the slightest smear of a hangover. He stopped by Mollin's last night to gift him with a bottle of Maker's and ended up hanging out long enough to make a big dent in it. Mollin told him he was thinking about selling the house and moving to Vegas.

"Dude, no," Joe said. "We're the last of the Burbank Mohicans."

"Shoulda put a ring on it," Mollin replied.

Joe readies himself to head out and open the bar. He showers and shaves, scrambles some eggs, and drinks a Bud Light and tomato juice.

Fonso, the old vato, is in his usual spot next to the front door of the building, his chair in a patch of sun on this chilly day. He's fifty-five but still dresses in a flannel shirt, pressed khakis, and Cortezes like he did when he was a teenager.

"*Feliz Navidad,* motherfucker," Joe says, and hands him his weekly twelve-pack, a white bow affixed to the box.

"Thanks, *ese,*" Fonso says. "You want to hit this?"

Joe waves off the spliff. He always turns down Fonso's weed. The guy talks way too much about angel dust, and Joe suspects he might dip his joints.

Football Sundays are busy from opening until the last game ends. This week Antoine is behind the bar with Joe. He's thirty, a clean-cut Black dude who went to USC and is now studying law online. He once showed Joe photos of himself from a catalog, wearing a turtleneck and tight pants. Joe suspects he's gay but hasn't given it much thought. He likes sharing shifts with him because he's all business, no bullshit.

The Scoreboard draws a different crowd than the Short Stop. Older, less hip. Fathers and sons come in, husbands and wives, whole families. This week there are lots of Santa hats, reindeer antlers, and ugly sweaters, but Joe's favorite Sunday regular, an old man everybody calls Mister, isn't down with that kind of foolishness. He takes his football seriously, showing up at noon every week and staying all day, sipping nonalcoholic beer. He has money on every game and is constantly phoning his bookie. Someone said he used to be an engineer at Lockheed, someone else said a college professor.

"Another O'Doul's?" Joe asks him.

"Not until this quarter ends," Mister says nervously, as if delivery of a beer at the wrong moment will jinx things for him. He's got a gambler's superstitiousness, ordering the same food every week—wings for lunch, a cheeseburger for dinner—and switching snapbacks from game to game, depending on which team he's betting.

Joe steps into the alley behind the bar for a cigarette. He plans on stopping at Von's on his way home and is putting together a list when his phone chirps. He's surprised to see a text from Emily. It must be a glitch in the system, an old message showing up months after it was sent. Part of him wants to delete it without opening it. He only recently stopped thinking about her at least once every day, and he can't see any good in going backward. Before he can fully form this thought, though, another part of him taps the text.

It's a video, stuff she shot during their trip, with an old Neil

Young song, "Like a Hurricane," playing over it. There's him pumping gas. There's the fire in the hills and Barstow. There's Emily filming herself staring out the truck's window at the desert. He chokes up but keeps watching. Vegas neon, sunset at the Grand Canyon, lightning in Lubbock. He was always looking straight ahead during the journey, focused on getting where they were going, but she was there to catch everything he missed, like a second set of eyes. When the video finishes, he's full of new regret.

He turns his brain off, though, and bulls his way through the rest of his shift. Night has fallen as cold and clear as fate by the time he leaves the bar. He drives aimlessly for a while, knowing only that he doesn't want to go back to his apartment, where the neighbors' fucking and fighting coming through the walls might finally break him. He ends up on the 101, then gets off on Las Virgenes headed toward the coast.

The dark, winding route downcanyon requires all his concentration. There are no taillights to follow, nobody else on the road. The gnarled scrub oaks and mesquite thickets flash like bone in the high beams. A buddy of his, drunk, hit a deer out here. The collision totaled his car and nearly killed him.

Joe knows he's getting close to Malibu when he starts seeing Christmas lights through the trees, houses decorated for the holiday. He drives south on PCH. He hasn't been out this way since that day with Emily. He pulls off the road at County Line and parks in the same lot they did.

Stars crowd the sky above the dead black ocean. Even so, it's so dark, he can barely make out the waves below. He feels like he's poised on the edge of the earth. A bunch of seagulls appears out of the darkness. He's never seen them flying at night and wonders if it means a storm is coming. He'd like to know such things.

He watches the video again. There's a shot of him and Emily reflected in a mirror in their room in Lubbock. They're in bed, him drinking a beer, her filming. She must have told him to smile and wave, because all of a sudden he does. *Look at those happy people,* he thinks, then remembers that by Lubbock, things were already coming apart. What he's watching are people wishing they were happy, people wanting to be happy, people pretending. The video ends with a single bat flapping out from under the bridge in Austin and spiraling up into the sky as the screen fades to black.

If Emily's sending him a coded message like the ones the lovers exchanged in *Anna Karenina,* he can't decipher it. "What do you do?" someone asked him once. "I put out fires," he replied. "Every day. With my bare hands." But maybe life won't always be like that. Maybe someday he'll have time to think, to piece together the puzzle of him and Emily, and then maybe he'll go looking for her.

Before driving back to the Valley, he texts her. *Where are you?* After a few days he stops waiting for a reply. Christmas passes. December turns into January. Winter warms into summer. His mom gets sick and gets better. He wrecks his truck and buys another.

August 15, 11:58 p.m.

I dreamed I was in love last night.

I know what kind of dream you're talking about.

It wasn't a dream about fucking, it was a dream about being happy. Me and this woman, this perfect woman. We were happy at the grocery store, happy at the laundromat, happy sitting on the couch, watching TV. I was happy to be with her, and she was happy to be with me. It was one of those dreams that seemed like it lasted all night. One of those where, when you wake up, it's like you've lived a whole other life. When I opened my eyes in the morning and figured out it wasn't real, I was so bummed, I almost cried.

What did your dream woman look like?

That's not what was important. What was important was the feeling I had for her. The fact I had it proved it exists somewhere inside me, which means there's a chance the dream could come true. You can't go looking for that kind of happiness though. That's how people fuck up. That's how I've fucked up, forcing or faking it. When that kind of happiness comes, *if* it comes, it'll come out of nowhere, and even if it doesn't last, it'll be enough to have had it for even just a while. I sail in rough seas, bro. A memory of something like that can keep you afloat. When everything else is fucked, a memory of something like that can save your life.

Acknowledgments

Thanks to Asya Muchnick and everybody at Mulholland/ Little, Brown who had a hand in producing this book. A special thanks to Joe Skyward, whose unique spirit animates this story and gives it life. Rest in Power, Chief.

About the Author

Richard Lange is the author of the story collections *Dead Boys* and *Sweet Nothing* and the novels *This Wicked World, Angel Baby, The Smack,* and *Rovers*. He is the recipient of a Guggenheim Fellowship, the International Association of Crime Writers' Hammett Prize, a Crime Writers' Association Dagger Award, and the Rosenthal Family Foundation Award from the American Academy of Arts and Letters. He lives in Los Angeles.